TA570912

SCION RISING

THE GUARDIANS OF LIGHT: BOOK 2

R. MICHAEL CARD

Gryphon's Gate Publishing

Scion Rising

Copyright © 2017 R. Michael Card

Gryphon's Gate Publishing

550 King St. N.

PO Box 42088 Conestoga

Waterloo, ON.

N2L 6K5

ebook ISBN978-1-988115-00-9

Print ISBN978-0-9937651-9-3

The night sang a discordant chorus of battle and Senia danced wildly to the tune.

The armies of The Blacklord had come to St. Antin Abbey. Within that fortress, the monks of Embreth and what remained of the forces of Hallania stood against them. The Blacklord's men outnumbered the allies by over twenty to one. The allied forces, however, had the strong walls of the abbey to guard them and a fully trained scion to defend them. All told, it was an even fight.

Senia leapt. Her massive sword, Emberthorn, blazed with living fire in her hands. From a distance, she might have seemed like a spark flashing up from the combat on the hills before the abbey. Hundreds of feet up and across, she sailed through the air, lazily flipping herself backward. She landed lightly, elegantly, on the fifty-foot wall of the abbey next to Ahrn.

Her lover used all of his fighting prowess to fling The Blacklord's magically enhanced, black-clad assassins off the wall. The assassins led the fight, jumping to the top of the walls and trying to clear a path for the hundreds of regular warriors with ropes and ladders waiting below.

A lull of battle around them gave enough time for her to lean in for a short but passionate kiss. She disengaged with a grin.

"How are the defenses?"

"Well enough. Two forces topped the wall in the past hour, but we rebuffed both."

"Keep up the good work."

"If you're heading out again, there's a Fire Wizard on that hill," He pointed, "who's been giving us some trouble."

Senia saw a stream of fire blowing from the hill in question to the top of the walls not far away.

"I'll give him some trouble then." Another grin and she was off, bounding from the wall, arching high over the battle to land on the hilltop.

The wizard, a woman, started at the sudden arrival of Senia before her. That hesitation was enough of an opportunity for Senia to spin in and slice her in twain, eliminating that threat.

For a moment, there was peace around her. The battle raged below her as The Blacklord's men surged forward around the hill she stood upon, but there were no threats here.

The allies held, but these nightly attacks wore away at the defenses and the hope of those within the abbey. Runners had been sent west to the nations of Fjoria, Scandia, and Nehrista, kingdoms to the west. Help had been promised, but it had yet to arrive. Senia feared without that help, despite her best efforts, The Blacklord's armies would probably overtake the walls of the abbey sometime before the end of the summer. She was doing her best, but they simply had far too many of the magical assassins and wizards for her to deal with, and more arrived daily.

She sighed and turned to leap back into the fray, but something stopped her.

It was an odd sensation, something she couldn't name.

She connected to the essence, the presence within her sword. *Emberthorn, what is that?*

I... it's been so long I can't be sure, but... Emberthorn's usually sure and steady baritone, which spoke within her mind, was hesitant.

But what?

There's an ability the monks mentioned in your training, one which they didn't talk much about as they figured it would never be used.

Senia racked her brain to remember, but the memory eluded her. *I...*

You have the ability to sense other scions, but I... I never thought... And this doesn't feel quite right either. It's been a while, but I'm sure I've never felt a scion that felt quite so...

Dark.

Yes.

Can you locate them?

I... yes. Actually... they're headed this way.

Indeed, the sensation, the pull, she felt toward this unknown source was moving, drawing nearer...

A moment later, descending from the night sky, a form landed on the hilltop near her, a tall, looming figure.

"Hello, Senia." His deep, resonant bass carried easily on the whispered breeze of the night. She didn't recognize the voice, nor what she could make out of him. He was quite tall, though his body was well proportioned so he did not seem 'lanky' as some taller men did . He was actually very well built, with thick, rolling muscles under his black shirt that accentuated his broad shoulders and wide chest. The fabric of his sleeves pulled tight over great, round biceps and forearms. Moonlight caught his features: sharp nose, heavy brow, rigid lines, strong jaw, framed by thick and full dark hair. He wore a smile that sent a chill down her spine. There was something about him that drew her, caught her and held her, yet another force equally as strong that scared her, shook her.

"Do I know you?" she said, wary. Though still there was a tingling within her that she somehow knew or should trust this man.

"You will, soon enough."

"Who are you?" she breathed.

"You can call me Davar." Several strides of his long legs brought him to within a sword's length distance. He looked her over, appraising. The gaze from those cold eyes enveloped her, powerful and dominating.

"What are you?" Senia asked.

"I've been sent to fetch you, bring you back... into the fold."

"Are there other scions?"

A pause. "Yes. Come with me and I'll show you."

No, don't.

I know he's lying, but how do I know? Why do I feel so sure I should trust this man and yet still somehow know he's lying?

I don't know.

"Perhaps," she said diplomatically. "At the moment however, I have a war to fight. Care to join me?"

He sighed, heaving round shoulders, eyes dark, piercing. "I didn't really think the ruse would work. If you can feel me the way I can feel you, then you already know—" He stopped himself short, as if coming too close to a flame. His next words were a mere breath, whispered. "Amazing. Such a shame."

With lightning speed, he reached back over his shoulder and drew a long dark blade that drank in the light around it and lunged at her.

She raised Emberthorn, blocking the strike, knocking it to the side. Yet the man's strength and speed were incredible. She had barely kept him from skewering her. Even now, in the blink of an eye before his next move, his blade hovered dangerously close to her side. She had only just managed to move it out of the way. The resistance against Emberthorn was immense. If this man wasn't a scion, he was certainly something she had never faced before.

He took a step back. His eyes ranged over her, measuring her.

She also stepped away, readying Emberthorn.

His blade was shorter, the length of a long broadsword, what some of the mercenaries called a hand-and-a-half sword or bastard sword. He held it easily in his left hand. She had the advantage when it came to blade length, but she had a sneaking suspicion he had the advantage when it came to knowing his opponent. He knew her, somehow, but she knew nothing of him or his capabilities.

You have no idea who this is? Why he's attacking me? She asked Emberthorn.

No, I'm just as confused as you. He is a scion... I think, but... Not.

I've never felt anything like him before.

Great.

He came in again, though it was clear within these first few strikes that he was testing her and the range of her weapon. He backed off again.

"Why are you doing this? Who are you?" she asked.

"I do what I must."

She had no idea what that meant. Her confusion was becoming a growing thread of fear. She did not like the power she sensed in this man.

He attacked in earnest.

His blade, swallowing light and dimming the area around them, was barely visible against the night, even more so for the speed with which he wielded it.

For a moment, she was on the defensive blocking his attacks. He was good, terrifyingly so. He was pushing her back, step by step. Since she'd bonded with Emberthorn no other man had ever felt a true threat, too slow, too weak, but Davar was... something else entirely.

She leapt, flipping back and away. In the air, she spotted a copse of trees behind her on the hilltop. A long branch reached out from one tree, and she landed on it, balancing easily.

"I warn you—" Her fear grew, and she needed time to

collect herself, but the rest of her words were cut off as he came flying at her in a leap of his own. Then they were both on the branch, engaged again, blades trimming the trees around them.

Davar knelt suddenly, shearing easily through the branch they stood on. Senia had been on the outer end and it fell from under her. She strengthened her legs and landed on her feet, but he was jumping down, blade slicing through the night. She blocked, but he feinted, moving his blade around hers, catching her on her left arm, cutting a shallow gash. The shock of someone actually landing a blow on her rang through Senia and Emberthorn.

This was wrong, so very wrong. She staggered away, swiping Emberthorn in front of her to back him off, but he leapt over the blade, striking down on her again. Senia, stunned by this move, failed to block, managing only to flinch to the side. His blade scored again, a light strike on her cheek, then a deeper cut across her upper chest and the bicep of her right arm.

Emberthorn's instincts took over, controlling her body, and she lashed out. But Davar's dark blade stopped the attack meant to shear him in two across his upper torso. It almost seemed as if it had been easy for him to block her heavier blade.

They stood there for a moment, close, her blade on his as she strained to end him. He simply smiled at her as he held Emberthorn at bay.

"They told me you would be harder than this." He didn't laugh, but there was mirth in his eyes. He was moving again, ducking under her blade, forcing it past him, then striking quickly at her thigh. Another hit, this one deep, the pain searing into her. Emberthorn's blazing spirit filled her with strength, keeping her upright, barely.

She was truly scared now, and a terror-born rage was burning within her. The flames licking along Emberthorn's blade turned a blazing blue as she retaliated. She attacked furiously, a blur of azure in the night. Davar was forced back, blocking and evading.

She used her reach advantage to keep him at bay, striking quickly yet keeping herself out of range. Finally, he leapt back, flinging himself to the far side of the hilltop. She hurled herself after him. She had the advantage, and she wouldn't give it away, nor would her fury allow him to escape, not now.

She descended upon him, Emberthorn slashing down, blue flames streaming in the dark. He blocked the blow, but the force of it sent him to one knee. He rolled away, coming to his feet with a quick and easy grace.

By all the gods! Was this what it was like to fight against her?

No, most people who fight you go down much easier. Emberthorn chimed in.

Ah.

She charged in.

He was set and ready, the expression on his chiseled features grim, dark.

She set upon him with all the skill and precision that her bond with Emberthorn and the past months of training allowed her. He backed up steadily now, blocking her blows, though she did score a hit to his forearm and another across his ribs.

She knew she had him, his blade was slowing. He had to be tiring. She lunged—

But he wasn't there.

It had been a lure, but she saw it far too late. He evaded the lunge, stepping to the side. He'd been backed up against a large tree and her blade slid easily through the thick trunk. She would have been able to withdraw it easily, given the heartbeat it would take to do so, but he didn't give her the time.

His blade came down onto her wrists. She saw the attack coming and barely had time to release Emberthorn and withdraw her hands... but that was a mistake she couldn't afford.

She'd been bonded with Emberthorn long enough that she retained much of her powers when not in contact with him, but she was still slower, if only a fraction. That was all he needed.

Even in the time it took her to say "Embertho—" to call the sword back to her hands, he spun and struck the flat of his blade hard against the side of her head.

She went down, vision blurring, the soft long grasses cushioning her little as she crashed to the ground.

"Ember..." She tried once again, but he struck her hard on the back of her head and her world spun into darkness.

CHAPTER 1

*W*yllea was sure she was going mad.

She'd seen her entire company slaughtered and was the only survivor. She'd been stranded behind enemy lines for nearly two months. She'd had one scant meal in the past three days and though she'd been able to find fresh water often enough, she was sure she would soon die from lack of food. And before she died, her mind would play tricks on her as it was now.

I'm not your mind playing tricks. I'm real.

She was sure that's what all the voices in crazy people's heads said. The trouble was she'd actually started responding to the voice. It had been getting stronger and stronger, harder to resist, over these past weeks as she'd tried to survive in a dark and barren land.

You're real? Not some figment of my imagination?

As real as the bow in your hand.

That's going a little far don't you think?

No, because I AM the bow in your hand.

You are the bow? I'm talking to a bow, a weapon. I'm talking to a bow inside my own head.

Yup, she was going crazy.

The other odd thing about the voice was... it wasn't any voice she recognized. She would have thought if she were creating some fantasy "self" to talk to in her head it would respond in her own voice or maybe that of her mother or someone she had known, but this voice she couldn't place. It was a woman's voice, strong and sure, low and resonant. She'd never heard any voice like it.

Wyllea, you are not going crazy! You must listen to me. I can help get us out of this mess!

Sure.

I can, if you'd just let me in.

Let you in? Aren't you already in? You've been bugging me for weeks now. I'd say that's pretty well in, don't you think?

No, I'm not. I'm in your head, yes, but that's not the same. Besides, it's taken me years of being by your side and then these past few weeks of your mind and body being so weak and strained that your natural defenses are down for me to speak to you this clearly. You need to let me in all the way, believe in me, who I am, what I can do. You need to bond with me.

Bond with you?

Really? This was where her crazy was taking her? Bonding to a voice in her head. She'd never been one for marriage, having spent her life as a mercenary. She'd had her fair share of men, some of whom she might have even considered laying aside her bow and settling down with if they'd ever wanted such things. But she'd never considered being with a woman, let alone bonding with one.

Especially if that woman was herself. That was just... crazy. Well, that explained it then.

Wyllea, please listen to me. I don't even know if it's possible, but I think it may be. I've never been able to speak to anyone like this before, not since my Guardian died and all of his line with him. I think perhaps...

Shut up, bow.

My name is Eaglewing.

Really? That's the name I've come up with for the voice in my head?

No, that's the name that was given to the bow in your hand. You've seen the images traced on it, the eagle in flight. That's me.

That's very logical of you, Eaglewing. In fact, I'm sure I've seen all those tracings. And perhaps with this bow being all I have left in the world I've seen them far too much lately, which is why I've associated the voice in my head to my bow. Yes, that makes sense.

Now you're the one talking crazy.

I'm pretty sure we're both crazy, actually.

Wyllea, please!

Shhh! Did you hear that?

What? Oh, yes. Sorry, you were distracting me. It sounds like... a hammer... hitting an anvil.

How would you know?

I've been around.

I'm not quite sure what that means. Now shut up, Eaglewing, and let me see what's going on.

Fine, but I'll be back. I'm not giving up on this.

I'm sure. Now, now shut up!

Wyllea was in a barren land and hadn't seen a village

in weeks. The Blacklord's men had pillaged and plundered these lands over a year ago. Crops reaped early to feed tens of thousands of men had had no one to replant them as the people here had also been taken. All that remained were fallow fields, black earth, and scavengers. Wyllea had kept herself close to water, knowing that much of survival, following a small river north and west toward Maalkin's Rise. She'd heard there were still those resisting The Blacklord in Hallania, north of the mountains, and hoped to join with them if she could slip past the front lines. On a clear day, she could see the mountains jutting up, gray and stark, to the north and west. She was fairly certain she was now in the land which had once been Vohria, but that still meant hundreds of miles to go to reach Hallania.

She was unsure she'd make it that far. She knew little of hunting. True, her aim with a bow was second to none; there simply wasn't any game to shoot. Three weeks ago she'd found a small refugee camp that had shared some food, but those were the last people she'd seen. With no easy food and no people to help her, she was going to die out here, alone. If there was a forge ahead, as the noise she'd heard suggested, that meant people and possibly help.

She'd been in a hillier land these last few days and there was a hill in front of her blocking her from seeing the true source of the noise. She crept up the hillside to peer over the top.

In the next valley was a small village. It sat on an east-west road, well paved and wide, which cut through the hills. There was a bridge over the river as well. She could see why The Blacklord's armies might keep this little village intact as a rest stop for messengers heading back to The Blacklord's realm or new recruits being sent to the front.

The sound she'd heard emanated from a squat building on the south side of the road with thick black smoke billowing from its chimney. A smithy would be another reason to keep the town intact. Not only was it a rest stop, but a place to fix weapons and armor, shoe horses, or make whatever other metalwork the army might need.

This brought up a very simple question for Wyllea, yet one very hard to answer: Should she go down to the village or avoid it?

Every fiber of her being said to avoid it. Every fiber that is, except her stomach.

"Maybe if I have a decent meal the voice will go away."

Don't count on it.

Shut up!

Eaglewing didn't reply, though strangely Wyllea got the vague impression of a sigh and a slow shake of the head.

This was really going too far. She needed a meal. She could risk the village... she hoped.

CHAPTER 2

Tirol nursed his ale. It wasn't great ale by any means. In fact, it wasn't even passable. It was swill, but when it was the only ale available, it was good enough.

Nothing was the same since The Blacklord's armies had taken these lands. Crops were stolen, food and drink confiscated, men of fighting age taken, women and girls also taken to keep the men happy. Only the old, infirm, and young remained and since they had little to eat—and most of what they did have was of poor quality—they tended to die rather quickly.

Prospects were not bright under The Blacklord's rule.

As a fit young man of fighting age, he'd managed to escape The Blacklord's press-gangs through a combination of luck, skill, and a large helping of cowardice. He was quite at home in the wild, so he'd run and hid. It was something he was good at. He wasn't proud of it, but he was alive and free, even if he was stuck behind enemy lines.

This was the first time in months he'd dared show his face in any town or village, and this one, despite being on the Trade Road, was so small he was sure no one would care about him. As long as he kept his head low and didn't cause trouble, he'd be fine.

So he nursed his ale in a dark corner of the small, dingy public house. There were four trestle tables in the center of the room and a couple of smaller square tables around the sides. He'd taken one in a corner away from the bar. He was tempted to order a second serving of what they called 'stew', but didn't want undue attention and that might seem out of place. Not that there was anyone else here to draw attention from. The room was empty save for the barkeep. Besides, he still wasn't sure exactly what the meat in the stew had been. His stomach was churning as it was. Though whether that was from the quality of the stew or because he hadn't eaten for days prior to this, he wasn't sure.

Someone entered the common room.

The light of day, stark and white against the darkness of the room, stung his eyes, and he couldn't make out who this newcomer was at first. He hoped it wasn't a Blacklord agent. When the door closed and the room was once again dark the newcomer became a deeper shadow in the dimness. He tried to make out what he could. They were draped in a great cloak which hid much, but... yes, he could make out the curve of full hips underneath the fabric. Yet this woman moved more like a man with strong, straight steps. She carried a bow. In these parts a weapon generally meant one thing: a warrior for The Blacklord.

The woman moved slowly, almost tentatively to the bar, which was really a long slab of wood sitting atop several casks. The hood of her cloak swayed from side to side. She was being cautious, assessing this place. That was certainly odd for a Blacklord agent. They weren't tentative at all. They took what they wanted.

"Food," the woman called out, her voice the final confirmation she was a she.

The barkeep, a fat man with a gimp leg and missing one eye, limped over to her. His reply was as verbose as her request had been.

"Money."

She produced some coins from within the cloak and slapped them onto the bar. He inspected them.

"These ain't Blacklord silver. Who are you, lassie?"

She slapped more coins down, and Tirol was sure he caught a glimpse of gold.

The barkeep looked at the gold and back at the woman. He licked his lips, then snatched up the small fortune and deposited it in his apron. "What will you have?"

"Bread, stew, whatever you have. Two servings and a stout ale."

The barkeep bobbed his head and went about gathering the requested items.

The woman turned, leaning against the bar, and used her time waiting to further inspect the room.

Tirol didn't look away fast enough when she turned to

him. He hoped the darkness of his corner hid his features, yet she seemed to peer at him for some time, seemingly seeing him quite well.

She whispered something, then shook her head and looked around the rest of the room, which was empty. She turned back to him.

Great. Attention, the last thing he wanted.

Unless she was pretty.

No! He reigned in that wild thought immediately. It didn't matter what she looked like if she was a Blacklord agent. Sure, she had used some foreign coins to pay for her meal, but that didn't say much. That could be loot taken from those she'd helped conquer. Better to stay away from her, no matter what she looked like.

Once the barkeep had provided her serving, she walked to his table, her steps slow, deliberate.

He couldn't catch a break.

She set her food down and sat across from him.

He'd picked this corner as it gave him a good view of the room, but now he found himself trapped. And so his life as a free man would come to an end. He shook his head slowly.

She pushed her hood back off her head, the motion catching his eyes. The look in her clear, green eyes was hard. Dark hair, matted and limp, framed a face with a slightly upturned nose and full lips. Despite the dirt on her, she was still the most attractive woman he'd seen in ages, even if she was here to take him in.

She said nothing, simply looked at him. After a moment, she brought a hunk of bread to her mouth and took a large bite. She chewed for a moment before stopping to inspect the bread and seeing the beginning of mold on it. She shrugged and continued to eat it.

Tirol had done the same thing, which instantly rang a bell in his head. This woman was hungry, really hungry. As hungry as he had been. That meant she wasn't getting regular meals, which she would be if she were a regular in The Blacklord's army. Looking closer in the gloom of the dark corner he caught sight of the leather armor she wore. Blacklord armor had a much higher neck-guard. Perhaps she wasn't with the enemy after all.

"You're no soldier," she said. It wasn't a question.

He was about to ask how she'd figured that out when she spoke again. "And since you're here instead of at the front, that makes you either a deserter or cunning."

Cunning. He liked the sound of that.

Here was the test. Was she trying to trap him and take him to the front or was she looking for a friend and ally against The Blacklord? He took a leap of faith.

"Cunning, yes," he whispered. He didn't wish the barkeep to overhear this conversation.

"Good." Now she too had lowered her voice, the soft sibilance teasing his ears. "Do you know these lands well?"

"I may." He still wasn't sure what he thought of her. Trust was not something that came easily to him.

Her next words were lower still, harsh, hissed, which seemed more for herself than for him. "How do you know —? Don't. Stop! I'm trying to talk to—" Her eyes caught his and she silenced herself. "Do you know a way over Maalkin's rise to Hallania?"

Not really, no. The mountains, despite not being overly high or treacherous, were simply not well explored. The range was not that large and there were many routes around them. Well, there *had* been many routes in the days before The Blacklord. But if she was looking for what he thought she was looking for, it wouldn't matter anyway.

"If you're hoping to sneak past the front lines, the mountains are no good. The front has already moved beyond them. The Blacklord has taken most of Hallania save the far west."

She cursed, and wasn't polite about it either. This was not a woman who'd had a gentle upbringing. She'd been around men, hard men, for some time to pick up language like that. The cursing told him what he needed to know, however. She was no Blacklord agent. She wanted away from this blasted place as much as he did.

That relaxed him a little. If she wasn't here to take him in then... well that led to a whole new set of possibilities.

Suddenly he couldn't help but notice her slender neck, her soft cheeks, and long fingers. She was a warrior, the bow and prolific cursing confirmed that, but she was a woman too. One unlike any he'd ever met before. She didn't simper, didn't cast moon eyes at him, certainly wasn't using any 'wiles' on him. She was addressing him straight, almost 'man-to-man', with confidence and grit.

And he liked it. You never knew where you stood with those simpering women, but with this one...

Perhaps...

"I may be able to get you past the front though." The words shocked him even though they were his own.

"Can you? How?"

Yes, that was an excellent question, one he was currently asking himself. He didn't know any such thing, yet apparently there was some idiotic part of him that wanted to help this woman, impress her. He had no idea why. Nor did he know exactly how that part had managed to overpower the usually much larger part of him concerned with safety and self-preservation.

Tirol was no idiot. He wasn't going to make the same mistake his father had made. He wasn't loyal, he wasn't self-sacrificing, and he didn't serve a cause. He served himself.

Yet somehow, he still didn't manage to stop himself from going on. "I've been hunting these lands since I was a boy. I've ranged all over Vohria, even into Aestria and Hallania. There are many hidden nooks or passes in these lands where a small group might pass unnoticed. Depending on how far west the front line has reached, I may just be able to find a good place for us to sneak through one of these secret places."

Her eyes studied him for some time. They were quite green, clear and bright. That much was evident even in the darkness of the corner they shared. Large verdant pools, like a forest pond on a sunny day.

When she spoke, it was slowly, crafting each word with those lush lips. "If you can get me past the front safely, I'll reward you... greatly."

He could already think of how he would take his reward. His self-preservation side, however, clamped down on those thoughts before he got too far. What was he doing mooning over some woman he'd just met and making promises he couldn't keep!

"My name is Tirol," he said extending a hand.

She took his in a strong grip. "Wyllea."

Wyllea... what a perfect name.

No, no it wasn't. It was a regular name! His self-preservation side kept trying to slap some sense into the rest of him, but to no avail. The rest of him was lost. Lost in the depths of brilliant green eyes.

CHAPTER 3

*T*wo days had passed, and the gnawing hunger was starting to seep back into Wyllea. Tirol had proven an adequate hunter, but he had no weapon to bring down larger prey, no bow—and she wasn't about to lend him hers or one of her last few arrows. So he'd hunted with a sling and they'd shared a rabbit the night before. But that meager fare was all they'd seen, and it hadn't been a fat rabbit.

He's trustworthy. You could lend me to him for hunting if you wish. You do need to eat.

How do you know we can trust him?

If you'd let me in fully, I'd share that with you. As it is, can't you sense it, even a little?

The sad part was that Wyllea could sense it. She didn't know where the notion was coming from, but it was like she could read this man's every gesture and glance and knew what he was thinking. She'd always had a bit of a special perception around people. At times in the past, she'd found she could tell what others were going to do before they did it, but this was a whole new level. She didn't know how or why, but she felt she could trust this man. That had been part of what had led her to him in that tavern. Then it had been but a notion, now it was a near surety. She could trust him.

See, I told you. Now if you'd bond with me, I could show you to do so much more! You'd understand everything I'm trying to do for you.

There you go about bonding again. I'm not going to bond with some voice in my head.

I'm the bow, remember. My name is Eaglewing!

I'm not going to bond with some bow!

I'm so very far from being "some bow," and besides, you'd be amazing as my Guardian!

"I said no." This came as a harsh whisper.

"What was that?" Tirol asked, walking beside her over the hilly countryside.

"Nothing." Gods! She was really going to have to watch her craziness around him. If he found out she was losing it, he might stop helping her. Sure, she was fine on her own. She'd been on her own for weeks before this, but she found herself reassured by the company. She'd always been around others, mostly men, and it felt good to have a companion again.

He won't stop helping you, at least not right away. He's too infatuated with you.

What, really?

Oh, yes. You have dazzled him with your 'beautiful green eyes'.

Wyllea blinked. The last time she'd gotten a good look at herself had been in the still waters of a brook before she drank. She really didn't think there was much to see—desperate and dirty. And that had been a while ago, so things couldn't have gotten better since then.

She took stock. Her... everything... was filthy: cloak, clothes, skin. Her hair was matted and limp. She'd never thought of herself as an attractive woman and truthfully had never cared much. She was a warrior, had been trained as such since she was old enough to hold a bow. Her father had had no sons, only her, and so she'd received the full force of his will to train her into the warrior he was. She had, in many ways, thought of herself more a man than a woman in most things. She'd been around men, and fighting men at that, for most of her life. They might have commented on her womanhood, until they saw her shoot or fight. Then they would shut up and she'd become one of them. What was there about her to be infatuated with?

Then it struck her... she was trying to refute an argument made by the crazy voice in her head. It was making stuff up. That's what crazy voices did.

I'm not making this up. Bond with me, and you'll see.

I'm not going to listen to you anymore.

Something caught her eye. On the next hill over she saw movement in black.

She caught Tirol's shoulder, hissing the word, "Down," and knelt, crouching low. Tirol had enough sense to do the same.

"What is it?" he whispered.

"I saw something up ahead. I think it's a Blacklord soldier. I'm going to check." She pressed her body to the earth and shimmied forward to the hilltop, peering out over the long grasses.

She'd been right. There was a sentry leaning on a spear atop the next hill. She wriggled back down to Tirol.

"I thought you said the front line was far to the west?"

"It is," he said evenly. "Why?"

"There's a sentry on the next hill. If it isn't their rear guard then..." What was he guarding? A slow grin spread over her face. "How fast can you run?"

"What, why? They haven't seen us have they?"

"We're not running away. We're running toward."

His face fell. "You're crazy!" he hissed, keeping his voice low.

She was pretty sure he wasn't referring to the voice in her head but her unorthodox plan. At least she hoped.

"Look, if their front lines are still far to the west then this fellow must be guarding a supply depot or something else of value. I want to get a closer look. I might just have a plan for an easier way to get us through the front lines, or at least something that might help us if we got caught."

"What are you thinking?" His tone made it clear he really didn't want to know. It was fairly obvious he wanted to be far away from anything to do with The Blacklord.

"I'll take down the guard. I have a clear shot, and at this distance, it shouldn't be a problem. But just in case anyone happens to be looking for that soldier standing on his hill, I need you to run over there once he's down and pick up his spear and stand there, looking guard-like. You're dressed in dark colors. From a distance, you should pass for a Blacklord soldier."

"I can't say I really like this plan. We don't need to do this. Why don't we just keep moving?"

"I'm the one paying you and I say we investigate. If we can get our hands on some Blacklord uniforms, that might help us later on."

He nodded halfheartedly. "I suppose…"

I just want to say that I'm against this plan. That guard is just doing his duty and…

Shut up. You get no say in this.

Again, she got the impression of Eaglewing sighing and shaking some nonexistent head.

"Are you ready?"

Tirol grimaced. "Sure, as ready as I'll ever be to go charging *toward* a Blacklord camp."

"Good. Go!"

He did, scrambling over the top of the hill and staying low.

She drew out an arrow, one of three remaining. That was another reason she wanted this raid. She needed ammunition.

You wouldn't need any ammunition if you bonded with me.

What? Really? How? Actually, never mind and shut up. You're distracting me.

She stood, nocked, and fired in one smooth motion. The arrow flew true to its target, taking the guard just under his chin, where little armor protected. He fell.

It seemed like an eternity before Tirol scrambled up to

take the guard's place, but it had been only a minute or two, so hopefully they were safe.

She jogged over to join him, staying low in the grass lest anyone happened to look their way and see two figures on the hill.

She peered into the next valley and smiled. "I was right, a supply dump."

"Great. So?"

"So now we resupply!"

"I was afraid you were going to say something like that."

"You like food don't you? Food that doesn't require hunting? Well, that's what's down there. Hopefully along with some uniforms and other things of use."

He grunted, not sounding pleased. "So what? We just march down there and take it? I don't think they'll like that."

"I need a moment to think."

He sighed and waited.

She studied the layout and distribution of men. "There are five men that I can see, possibly more inside the tents. Also probably a few more sentries on other hills." She peered around at the hills surrounding the camp and indeed picked out three other figures with her exceptional distance sight. "It'll be easiest if we wait until nightfall. We can use the darkness to sneak in."

"Great, so I have to stand here for several more hours? Why didn't you wait for nightfall before you attacked the sentry? Then we could sneak right in."

"I..." That would have been wiser. Oh well. She always

had been a little quick to act. "You're probably right, but we're here now so we have to make the best of it. All you have to do is stand there until sundown. Shouldn't be too hard." A thought occurred to her. "Unless they send someone to relieve you. In which case, you'd have to go down earlier."

"Care to explain that plan in a little more detail? How would them sending someone out to relieve me mean I go in?"

"Because if they send someone out, they'll expect someone back."

"Ah, and what will we do with the someone they send?"

"Same thing we did with this guy," she said plucking her arrow, still good, from the body of the sentry. She cleaned it and put it back in her quiver. "I'll take him out and take his place, standing on the hill, but you'll need to go down in the place of the sentry that was to be relieved." She took another look at the dead body before her and stripped off its sword belt. "Here, this might help." She handed it over to him.

"Why can't you go?" He strapped on the sword belt. "It's not like I know how to use one of these particularly well. I'm a hunter not a warrior."

"I could, depending on how dark it gets, but you're much more likely to pass as a random man than I am."

"I suppose. Have I mentioned how much I don't like this idea?"

"Yes. Now shut up and wait."

Tirol grimaced.

CHAPTER 4

*T*he sun hovered just over the horizon in the west. Not too much time had passed, but it felt like an eternity to Tirol, standing exposed on the top of the hill.

He was beginning to rethink his arrangement with this warrior woman. Perhaps she'd spent too much time alone in the wild. This whole idea of attacking and raiding an enemy camp where they were outnumbered at least five to one and their only real weapon was her bow didn't sit well with him. Sure he had a sword now, but he'd never felt all that comfortable with such a weapon. He preferred stealth and subtlety to confrontation.

He was starting to think he should have listened to his self-preservation when it warned him not to get involved with her. He was not his father, after all. He wasn't about to sacrifice himself for anything. He couldn't understand why anyone would do such a thing. Why would a loving father abandon his family to fight in a war he couldn't win? What sense did that make? Why would any man care about anything other than himself and his kin?

His logic won.

"Wyllea, I'm done. I can't—"

"Hush, someone is coming."

He'd waited too long. Now he was committed. He just shook his head and sighed. "What do I do?"

"What you're doing. Just stand there and answer if this guy calls out."

"Easy enough." Too bad it was all still crazy.

Wyllea crouched, drew an arrow from a quiver on her hip, and nocked it. She only had two other arrows in the quiver. Yup, she was crazy.

"You expect to pull this off with only three arrows?" He tried to put as much scorn and incredulity into his voice as possible.

"Shut up, he's getting closer. And yes, I do."

"Ho there, Ylvin!" Came a call from behind Tirol. "Sundown's nearly upon us. Time to go and get some food and rest."

"He sounds nice," Tirol whispered.

"Say something back," Wyllea hissed.

"Sounds good!" Tirol called out, half turning.

"Ylvin?"

Wyllea drew back the arrow and let fly. Tirol heard a wet thunk, then the thud which he assumed was a body hitting the ground.

"Get him over the hill, quickly!" she said, drawing another arrow and scanning the camp and surrounding hills. Tirol did as commanded, turning and running down the hill to the fallen man who was most thoroughly dead, then dragging him up the hill and over. Gods, but he wasn't used to this level of exertion! He was panting hard by the time he dropped the body.

She swore. "You didn't even try to preserve the arrow, did you?"

"What?" Gods, but she was infuriating.

"Never mind," Wyllea said, stripping the sword belt off the new body and strapping it on. Then she stood, taking his spear. "It'll be dark soon. The sun is almost down. You go down into the camp and look around, scout things out. I'll be down as soon as it's dark enough. Find the supply tent, we'll meet there."

"I said two words to this last guy and he suspected me. What makes you think I'll last two minutes down there if they can actually see me?"

"You said you were a hunter. Hunters are skilled at evading prey and not being seen, so do that."

"I wasn't really the best hunter, actually. I—"

"Are you going or not?" She was gazing at him with those large green eyes again. There was something about her, an intensity that seemed to sing through her body and everything she did. It was in her eyes now, holding him. Gods, but it was intoxicating.

His anger faded. "Yes," he said.

No! His ingrained self-preservation screamed at him to run, but he wouldn't. He had no clue why, but he would have done anything for Wyllea in that moment.

He made his way down the hill, grumbling all the way, arguing with himself. He took the sword he'd stolen from the first guard out of its sheath and tested it. It was fairly well-balanced and didn't feel too awkward. He'd been forced to use similar swords before. He could hold his own with one but would prefer not to have to.

So he kept his eyes open.

There were three men at one end of the camp, two by a cooking fire, another moving back and forth between the fire and a single small tent. That was good. With the growing dark, the night vision of those by the fire would be horrible. If he could keep out of sight until full dark, he'd be fine.

Reaching inside his tunic, he drew out a small pouch. It was light, almost empty, causing him to grimace and sigh. This was his preferred means of dealing with confrontation. A potent powder that, when blown in someone's face, caused them to become disoriented and fall asleep. He'd purchased it from a witch-woman in Vohrial. Not only was the city hundreds of miles away, but it had been destroyed by The Blacklord's armies. So this powder would be very hard to replace once gone, and judging from the weight, there were probably only two or three uses left. Still, he'd rather use it than a sword, so he sheathed his weapon and kept the pouch in his hand, ready if needed.

He'd kept the existence of his powder a secret just as he hadn't been fully honest with Wyllea by saying he was a hunter. Sure, he'd been a hunter. He'd done many things. But before the war, the prey he'd been hunting were the precious items the wealthy kept locked away. He'd had a good run, amassing a small horde of goods pilfered from the richer residents of Vohrial. His sleeping powder had helped him escape more than one angry lord or persistent city guard, and he hoped it would help him survive this night as well.

He chided himself again. Now that he was away from Wyllea, it was easier. If he survived this raid, he was going his own way. He'd be his own man once more. He didn't need her or her reward whatever it may be.

He should just walk away right now.

He should... but he didn't.

Tirol had made his way around the camp to the opposite side from where the three men shared a fire to one of the large tents which he hoped held food and supplies.

He was nearing the opening when it was pushed aside and a guard walked out. The man hadn't expected anyone to be there and almost walked into Tirol. This gave Tirol the chance to pluck some dust from his bag and blow it in the man's face.

The guard looked surprised, then his eyes drooped shut and he slumped to the ground.

Tirol was left shaking and breathing hard. Gods, but this was such a stupid idea.

He turned to walk away but took no steps.

He turned back.

Then turned away again.

Why was this so difficult! He was his own man. He was not going to sacrifice himself like his father. He would not abandon all he held dear for some cause! Especially not for those brilliant green eyes... or that slender neck and dark hair... or those full lips and that curvaceous body.

He turned back. He was a fool, and that was it. A fool for a pretty face.

He hefted the guard's body and dragged it around to the side of the tent. The guard should be out for a good few hours. Then Tirol went back and entered the supply tent.

And froze.

"Pollan, is that you?" said a guard sitting at a desk not five feet away. The man started to turn. "Back with supper so soon?"

But Tirol was quicker and ducked behind a shelf piled high with sacks and small crates without a sound. He stood deathly still and waited.

"Pollan?" Between the sacks, Tirol watched the guard.

The man peered at the opening of the tent for a moment, then shrugged and turned back to his desk.

Tirol allowed himself to breathe again. Though he had to admit his situation wasn't good, stuck in a tent with at least one guard whose hearing was fairly good.

Great.

He should have walked away. But he was in it now and might as well follow through. Carefully he drew the short sword Wyllea had given him. He would have preferred to use his sleeping powder, but with the man facing away from him, it might not work as well, and the last thing he wanted was to make the guard turn around in order to get a better angle on him. Too much could go wrong with that idea. No. As messy as it was, it would be better to stab the guy in the back or some other unsavory attack: quick, quiet, and deadly.

He snuck from behind the shelf and stalked to the man at the desk, who seemed intent on some ledgers in which he was scrawling away. Many years as a thief had honed Tirol's ability to move without a sound.

Tirol was so quiet that he had a moment, standing behind the doomed clerk, to ponder his actions. The man wore no armor, though he wore the uniform of The Blacklord. Tirol knew that many of The Blacklord's minions were once just ordinary people of far-flung lands, conquered and given the choice to serve or die. And yet these were the people who had killed his father so many years ago. This man didn't seem to be forced to do his duties. Tirol couldn't fathom what it would take for someone to give up freedom so easily.

Perhaps he'd give this man a chance.

With one quick motion, he reached around the man's head with both arms, one clamping over the man's mouth, the other bringing his sword to the man's neck.

The man struggled, but only for a moment, until the surprise must have worn off.

Tirol leaned down, his mouth close to the man's ear. "Do you serve The Blacklord willingly?" he asked, keeping his voice low, husky, masked so that if this man survived and someone didn't see Tirol, he might avoid detection.

The man shook his head.

"Then you have two options, my friend. Either I kill you now, or I grant you your freedom. You can run, keeping quiet, and live free. I know we're behind the front lines and there are Blacklord men everywhere, but at least you'd have a chance out there in the wild. So what will it be? Nod if you want to live."

The man nodded, vigorously.

"I'm going to remove my hand from your mouth. Make a sound or any quick movement, and you die. Understand?"

Another nod.

Tirol removed his hand.

The man began to turn, but Tirol stopped him with his now free hand, pushing his head back facing forward. "I would prefer if you didn't see me."

"I won't look," the man whispered. "What should I do?"

"Do you have any family?"

"No."

"Then go where you wish. There are enough gaps in the front lines you should be able to sneak through if you can keep yourself hidden. Go ahead, steal some food, and run. Keep low in the valleys close to water, and you should be fine. Understand?"

"Yes."

Tirol moved his sword, sliding it carefully back to the man's shoulder, then down his back, always keeping contact.

"Stand."

The man stood. Tirol kicked his stool aside.

"Move slowly. Grab what you will and then get out. I'll be right behind you the whole way. If you make any move to yell, I'll run you through."

"I won't," the man said, taking his time to turn. Tirol kept tension on his sword and followed the man as he moved to a shelf. He opened a bag and grabbed several small parchment-wrapped items, took some slices of dried fruit from another bag, a small wheel of cheese from yet another. Then he turned to the door and moved carefully toward it.

This was the perilous part. Once outside, the man could do as he wished. Tirol could only hope the man was smart enough to run.

The man stopped at the flap to the tent and said only, "Thank you," then moved out into the night.

Tirol waited for a call, some alarm, but none came.

Apparently, luck was on his side tonight.

He turned, now knowing where food was located, and started toward the shelves, but the flap on the other side of the tent opened and a guard stepped in.

"Handar, is that you? Hadn't seen you or Pollan at supper and..."

The light was dim, only two candles on the desk burning, and Tirol was of a height with the man he'd just freed, but he knew any confusion wouldn't last long, so he charged the guard.

The man didn't call out, just stood there stunned as Tirol bowled into him. The motion knocked them out of the tent, and they ended up on the ground.

Tirol was no stranger to a rough-and-tumble brawl and got in a few good punches to the man's face before the other recovered from his surprise and began fighting back in earnest. He was larger than Tirol and hit harder. The first hit stunned him, the second left his head ringing, and the third threw him off the guard, rolling to the ground.

Great.

This was how he was going to die: so close to so much food, in the dark, far from home.

The other man stood and kicked Tirol in the gut, doubling him over and making him cough. The guard moved his foot back to kick again and—

—fell limp to the ground next to Tirol, an arrow in his back.

A moment later Wyllea was next to him. "Can you stand?" she whispered. He could swear there was genuine concern in her voice.

When he didn't respond fast enough, she said, "Tirol? How are you?"

He rolled to his hands and knees. This made his stomach churn with displeasure and sent his head spinning, but they settled after a moment. "I'll be fine. I've taken worse."

"Thank, Reisha! Come on, get up. I don't know if anyone heard that fight or not. We need to get out of sight."

He nodded and rose, slowly staggering back into the tent. Wyllea, apparently stronger than she looked, dragged the fallen guard in after them.

Tirol stumbled over to the desk and leaned on it, waiting for his head to clear fully and his body to start responding the way it should. He felt around where he'd been kicked, but the man had gotten the soft part of the belly, no ribs.

Wyllea came to him a moment later. "I think we're good. Find anything?"

Tirol took his time, drawing a long breath and letting it

out. He was starting to feel better, but not whole yet. He forced himself to stand upright and turned to her, nodding.

"Yes, this way." He showed her the bags of food, and they packed away a small hoard for themselves in two large rucksacks with straps so they could be worn on the back. They also found blankets for a bedroll and tied those to their packs. Then Wyllea started hunting for more. She searched around the rest of the shelves for a moment but came back, grumbling.

"There are no arrows here, only food and clothes and such. Speaking of which, put this on." She handed him a bundle. "I'm going to see if the next tent over has any ammunition." She turned and left.

Tirol changed. It was a Blacklord uniform with a padded gambeson and breeches. It was made so plate or chain armor could be worn over-top, but both would slow Tirol down more than he liked, so he didn't even try searching for any armor. There was a cloak with a hood as well.

Wyllea returned a moment later, smiling, with three quivers tucked under one arm.

"Are we good? Can we go now?" Tirol whispered.

"One moment. My turn." She dropped her items and proceeded to strip off her clothes.

He hadn't really seen much under her great cloak, and when it fell away along with the layers beneath he was pleasantly surprised. That was until he remembered about modesty and turned around quickly.

Yet the image of her stuck in his mind like a burr. Her

dark hair, if not black then close to it, fell to just below her collarbone, brushing well-shaped shoulders and arms honed from years with a bow. Her shift clung to her form, revealing a curvy figure, full bosom, slender waist, and round hips. The shift cut off mid thigh, and her legs were firm, strong, and shapely. Overall, quite the picture of womanhood—even if she didn't act the part of any woman he knew.

She tapped him on the shoulder, now stepping close behind him. "What?" she said playfully. "Didn't like what you saw?"

Oh, he liked it well enough.

"I thought one of us should consider your modesty," he said evenly.

"Such a gentleman." She moved around him, now fully dressed, one of the quivers at her waist, the other two tied to her pack. "Ready to go?"

He was, and they did.

They slipped off into the night, quiet as the thieves they were, and Tirol could not get over the amount of good fortune that had befallen them. Perhaps she was a charm for luck. Maybe he should stay with her. He tried to convince himself that was the reason he didn't run off on his own, not the lingering image of her stripped down.

Tried and failed.

CHAPTER 5

*W*ithout much food in her, Wyllea grew tired quickly, but they kept moving for most of the night, putting as much distance between themselves and the supply camp as possible. By the time the moon had set, she figured they were far enough away and they stopped to rest. Tirol complained about still feeling energized from the raid and the running, unsure if he'd sleep, but Wyllea wrapped herself in her new warm blanket and was soon out cold.

They woke late the next day.

The sun had begun to warm the crisp morning air of a northern summer morning. Wyllea was used to more southerly climes, and these cool summer mornings, though not unpleasant, were far from the heat of the south she had once known. However, the day grew warmer with each passing moment she stayed under her blankets, enjoying the sun on her face. It could just turn out to be a good day.

They walked for some time then stopped by a wide creek to indulge in a lunch from their new stores. The parchment packages contained hard salted meat, tangy and tough, but wonderful as far as Wyllea was concerned. The dried fruit was sweet and chewy, and the cheese was pungent and slightly crumbly. It was the best meal she'd had in weeks, maybe months.

She ate her fill, then rose, moving toward the creek. "I'm going to bathe. New clothes deserve a clean body."

"Not a bad idea," Tirol said, nodding. "Shall I go downstream a ways?"

"Why?"

"To bathe."

She laughed as she undid the laces of her gambeson. "You still think I need to worry about my modesty? I've been in the army since I was seventeen, as soon as I was able to hit a target at five hundred paces. There's no room for modesty in the army. I've bathed with men around me most of my life. It's no problem for me."

"Ah," he said, drawing out the sound. Then he blew out a breath. "I suppose it would be safer if we stayed close."

"It would." She wasn't going to coddle him. He could make his own decisions. They'd been moving toward the creek as they talked, and reaching the rocky bank she lifted off her gambeson and lay it on some rocks so it wouldn't get too dirty. Then she undid her breeches and removed them, laying them next to the padded shirt. She then shrugged out of her shift and underclothes but kept them in hand. They needed washing and would go in with her. She picked up Eaglewing and brought her into the creek a bit, laying her on a few rocks close to where she would bathe.

Wyllea did her best to ignore the ramblings of the bow in her head. She'd apparently accepted that it was the bow speaking to her, which was just as crazy as her speaking to herself; in fact, it seemed to make it easier to distance herself from the near constant chatter. Over the morning, the bow had been going on and on about some call for help and someone needing assistance. This made no sense, so she'd done what she could to tune it out.

Once the bow was out of her hands the voice dimmed, seeming distant, and as she moved away, wading into the stream, it grew quieter still. Eaglewing was an exceptional bow, and there was no way Wyllea would ever willingly give her up, but it was nice to get away from the noise.

The water was crisp and cold, causing gooseflesh all over. She found a spot with a firm, sandy bottom and decided that would do. The water only reached to her mid stomach, but that was deep enough.

Curious, she glanced over at Tirol.

He had stripped off his clothes and was wading in, slightly downstream. He was a fair image of a man. Not as big or muscular as most of the men she'd known in the army, but tall and lean with firm-enough muscles.

She watched certain tender parts of him shrink as he waded deeper into the water and smirked. She couldn't help but call out, "Cold enough, isn't it!"

He looked over at her and froze. "Wha—? Ah, sure,

yeah," he stammered. Then he quickly turned away. The quick movement must have caused him to step on some slippery rock or other, for he then fell backward into the creek. He came up sputtering, and she laughed.

He looked over again then away just as quickly.

Gods, but he was a modest one. You'd think he'd never seen a woman before.

She couldn't help but chuckle to herself as she washed her undergarments, using stone and sand to get most of the sweat and dirt out of them. Then she dipped herself into the cold waters, scrubbing sand over her body and doing her best to rinse her hair.

When she waded out, the sun was warm on her skin, and she wiped off the water as best she could so the sun could dry her quicker.

Tirol was already out and dressing. He looked like he was still a bit damp, but she had no desire to get dressed while still wet.

"What's the hurry?" she called to him, and just as before, he glanced over, seemed to freeze for a moment, then looked away.

"Just want to get warm," he called back.

She grinned as his discomfort. Something about making him squirm with his modesty seemed infinitely funny to her. Her mood still light, she found a long flat rock to lie on. The stone was well warmed by the sun, and it was pleasant to stretch herself out in the heat, drying. She could only imagine what Tirol would think of her laying nude in the sun. The thought made her laugh again. He was an odd one, but she had to admit he'd done well on the raid and held his own. And having seen him naked, he didn't have anything to be ashamed of. She wasn't sure why he seemed so flustered around her. She shrugged the thought off and enjoyed her sunning. There were probably going to be many rough days ahead. You had to learn to enjoy the good ones.

When she finally rose, dry and warm, she found Tirol sitting by their camp, facing away from her. She dressed and picked up Eaglewing.

Wyllea, you must help!

The call was so strong it nearly brought her to her knees. It took every shred of will she had to ignore the flurry of words and emotions bashing against her from the bow as she walked the short distance to their camp. Could the bow actually be trying to talk to her? Was it possible she wasn't going mad, just that her bow had somehow gained intelligence and emotion?

It seemed absolutely preposterous. And yet...

She set Eaglewing down and sat several feet away. If Tirol thought this odd, he didn't comment. Apparently, her teasing of the man had been too much, and he was refusing to speak to her. At least that was the best explanation she could come up with for the man's silence.

When they moved on that afternoon, Tirol walked ahead of her. The short distance between them seemed greater for his refusal to speak to her. It was starting to be annoying. But it was only one of many annoyances. In a way, Wyllea was glad Tirol was in front. It meant he didn't see her constant struggle to remain in control over the bow, which beat at her with such an intensity she could barely control it. It raged and shouted at her to help, that there was someone out there who needed them. It was all Wyllea could do to simply keep putting one foot in front of the other. She wondered what might happen if she did indeed fail to stem this tide of emotion? What would become of her if she lost control?

CHAPTER 6

*T*irol sat, staring at the fire as night deepened around him, long after Wyllea had finished her meal and rolled herself up in her blankets.

He couldn't get the image of her body out of his head. It hadn't helped that she'd tormented him back at the river, calling to him again and again as she stood there nude.

It wasn't like he hadn't seen other women's bodies before. He'd bedded his fair share of maidens in his time, but none of them had flaunted themselves in quite the same way as Wyllea had. Most of the women he'd known had remained half dressed while they'd been with him. Some had had rather exceptional bodies and weren't afraid to show off in private, but even they didn't run around naked just anywhere. They might wear a dress that showed a lot of cleavage or most of a calf, but the rest they revealed only in private and never quite as brazenly as Wyllea did. Strutting around nude on the banks of the creek for the entire world to see. Not that anyone other than him had seen, but still!

What sort of woman was she?

She'd admitted she had no modesty, that her time in the army surrounded by men had stripped that from her, but...

He sighed.

If he was honest, he knew the problem wasn't with her.

He'd acted so foolishly, constantly turning away, then realizing he didn't have to but feeling too awkward to look back. His own meager modesty had tripped him up more times today than he wanted to admit. She just befuddled him so much!

If she was any other woman doing the things she did, perhaps he would have watched, but Wyllea was... different. He didn't know how exactly or why she twisted him up inside to the point that he could think of nothing but her, but she did.

With another heavy sigh, he figured he might as well try to get some sleep.

The night was warm and he might have been fine just laying dressed atop his blankets, but he felt the need for comfort and bundled himself tightly in the thick cloth.

～

A mist lay heavy around him in the night. The moon shone brightly, illuminating the fine moisture. It was pristine, perfect.

He couldn't shake the remembrance of Wyllea in the

river that afternoon, her body so perfect in proportion, her manner so open and free. She was everything he might ever want in a woman, and at the same time everything he was certain he would never have. She was intoxicating, making him feel excited and ill, all at the same time.

Then, like a wraith in the night, she was there. She stood beside his blankets, though how she had moved so keenly, without a sound, he knew not. Yet that thought faded quickly, for she stood before him naked, as she had been when bathing. He marveled again at her form, ideal in every way, her strong, shapely calves and thighs, round hips, slender waist, full high breasts, arms lean and sculpted, and a face like none he could have imagined. Now that the grime and dirt were gone and her hair washed and no longer matted, she was more than beautiful, radiant. Her hair fell in waves to her shoulders, framing a slender face, brilliant green eyes, straight nose, and wide, full lips. She was smiling at him.

"I know what you want," she breathed, and the faint words filtered down to him. Did she really know? Could she know his feelings, his desires, how he longed to be with her?

She knelt beside him, moving his blankets away, caressing the bare skin beneath. Her hand came to his face, cupping it. She bent lower pressing her lips to his, her tongue emerging, seeking, sucking the breath from him. Far too soon, it was over, but the intensity of the action told him clear enough how she felt, her own need.

Then she was next to him, laying her body, both soft and hard, beside his. She pressed closer for another kiss, longer, deeper. His hand found the curve of a breast and kneaded it roughly, following her lead. A moan from deep within escaped her lips. They lingered there, in the enchantment of their mutual caress, as Tirol could only marvel at his fortune.

Then she moved, straddled him, taking control.

Tirol's marvel turned to bliss and he lost himself in it. His hands strayed and stroke her smooth, warm flesh, moving on their own. Passions mounted as this moment of purest pleasure built in waves. he let himself drift on the tide of their desire, higher and higher, until it came crashing on the shores of paradise.

Voices cried out into the night, hers and his. He didn't seem to know himself. He had so fully merged with her and she with him. They were one mind and soul mingled within a sweat-soaked heap of flesh, quivering in the mist.

The dream ended suddenly.

Tirol woke with a gasp.

CHAPTER 7

*W*yllea woke in the night, her body warm, tingling.

Gods but that had been a vivid dream!

Her body trembled, blissful, from the remembrance. It had been so odd, like she wasn't in control of her own body. Such things weren't uncommon in dreams, though what she'd been doing was not a common dream for her by any means, and with Tirol no less. It had felt so real, so delightfully real. She may not have been in control of her body, but she'd certainly taken control in the dream, demanding, leading, and ultimately getting everything she desired.

Her body quivered again, warming. Gods! She threw off some blankets and sprawled, hoping to cool herself. In doing so, her hand brushed Eaglewing.

HELP NOW, PLEASE!

Like a cold bucket of water dumped over her, the call

resonated through her, dispelling any lingering effects from the dream.

Will you not be quiet! Wyllea yelled back, though the concept of yelling within her own thoughts was slightly baffling.

Please, Wyllea, please. You must help. Senia is in grave danger!

Who in all the blazes of the deep is Senia? And why should I care?

She's a scion.

A what?

A true-blooded descendant of the Guardians of Aehryn.

I repeat, a what?

Wyllea, just stop being so stubborn and listen to me!

Wyllea actually thought about this for a moment. If, and it was a massive 'if,' she wasn't going crazy. If this was her bow finding some way to communicate with her—which had a whole other set of very implausible 'ifs' attached to it, including if bows could possibly have intelligence—and if there was some person out there that needed her help, what would she do?

Boiled down, it came to this: someone might need her help. Would she provide it?

Yes, she would. That's what she had been trained to do in her years as a soldier. That wasn't the real issue though. The real issue was would she follow what might possibly be some random crazy thought?

Have I ever lied to you or led you astray?

Well...

Have I not always shot true? Have I not warned you of

dangers, kept you safe, as I did for your father and his father and back for generations?

I suppose so.

Then...?

Wyllea sighed heavily. *I'll go.*

Oh, thank you, Wyllea. I didn't want to have to compel you.

You can do that?

I can now. We've had a deep enough connection for long enough, yet it's the last thing I would want to do.

Good to know. Can this wait for morning?

I think so. The call that I'm getting is still to the west. They're moving east quickly, but they are also a fair ways north of us. If we head north from here, we should meet up with them.

Then tomorrow we'll go after them.

I'll guide you. Thank you again, Wyllea. You will not regret this.

I already do. You snapped me out of a rather pleasant memory of a dream, you know.

Oh, that. You should be careful about that.

What? Dreaming?

No, getting too deep. I didn't think you had acquired that much ability from me, but if you have, you need to be wary of playing with others' thoughts.

Playing with others' thoughts?

Well in this case, you weren't in control, but you did join with him. It was his dream, but you were deep in his thoughts. That's a dangerous place. If you lose control, you can get lost, and if you take too much control, you can drive a person mad.

None of that makes any sense. It had been her dream, had it not? Yet the bow had said, "it was his dream." But "him" who? Tirol? She'd been in his dream? No. How could that happen?

She gave a soft laugh at the thought. If it had been his dream, he sure knew how to handle a woman. She felt another shudder of pleasure at the remembrance. No, it must have been just a normal dream. Any alternative was simply absurd.

Wyllea felt Eaglewing's frustration. *It wouldn't be absurd if we were bonded. There is so much you could do!*

Ah, well, if I have my way, we'll stay not bonded.

Why?

That's a big obligation you're talking about. I'd rather stay free and in control of my own destiny, thanks.

We shall see Wyllea. We shall see.

CHAPTER 8

Tirol's emotions wouldn't settle. They heaved and tossed and frothed within him. His dream from the previous night was driving him mad with frustration. On the one hand, it had been an amazing moment—even if it had been a dream—and he didn't want to let it go. On the other hand, it hadn't been real, only the sad imaginings of a man lost in a boyish infatuation. Wyllea didn't want him like that.

Did she?

She certainly had never given him any sign or said anything to that end. If she'd lost her modesty living around rough men, then she'd probably had those rough men in her bed at some point. He was sure that's what she wanted, a man who could take control, and that wasn't him. He wasn't rough and strong and sure. He was subtle and quiet and cunning. So she'd remain only a dream to him. A thought which burned with disappointment and resentment. The joy of the dream had now long faded, overcome by aggravation that it would never be more than a delusion and anger at himself for being this out of sorts for a woman. Add to that his new uncertainty about where they were heading and why, and he was feeling more than a little testy this morning.

"Where are we going, exactly?" he asked, again.

"North." Which had been her reply every time.

Gods, but this woman was infuriating! He'd never known a woman who could drive him crazy with desire and with distress at the same time.

"And you won't say why? The front lines are west. The only thing north are the mountains."

"Trust me."

He was wearing a little thin on trust at the moment.

He gritted his teeth and followed.

He should just walk away. It wasn't the first time he'd considered it that day. The problem was he couldn't. The mere possibility that she might like him, might in some distant future be the woman from his dream and share the passion he now knew he felt for her, that ever-so-slight chance kept him with her. His self-preservation was telling him it was foolish to think she might change, might want to be with him, but he was ignoring it. His father had left the people he cared for, but Tirol would not do the same.

So he grumbled to himself and plodded along... north.

They were climbing into higher and higher foothills, and just before midday Wyllea stopped.

"What is it?" he asked.

"People ahead."

Tirol looked around. They were on the upslope of a hill, and the only thing he saw ahead was the top of that hill covered in long grasses. "Where?"

"The next valley." After a moment, she awkwardly added, "I hear them."

Tirol strained his hearing. He'd always had good ears, trained from years of working in darkness, pilfering the rich in Vohrial. He heard nothing.

"I..."

She cut him off with a "shush" and began creeping toward the top of the hill. He followed in a similar manner.

At the peak of the hill, they peered down into what looked like an abandoned camp. There was a small forest filling the valley to their east. A stream emerged from the forest and cut along the valley floor, disappearing around a bend to the west. Next to the stream, three recently doused fires still smoked.

"I think your ears are playing tricks on you," Tirol said, looking for anyone in the valley and seeing no movement.

"No, there are people. They're close, getting closer still. I don't know how they know we're here, but..."

"How do you know any of this?"

"I... can't explain. Not now. Someone's coming."

Tirol listened again. He heard nothing but the grasses sighing in the wind.

"Stand and show yourselves!" came a command from off to their right.

Wyllea swore. She whispered, "Act like a soldier. You're dressed for the part." Then she stood slowly.

This was all wrong. None of this made any sense. He

rose to see a man clad in black standing less than thirty feet away. Suddenly Tirol understood how the man had gotten so close without a sound. He was an assassin. A man gifted by The Blacklord with special powers of strength and speed and more. His attire gave him away, the loose black clothing with a wrap around his head so only his eyes showed.

This was not good. Tirol put the pieces together quickly: an empty camp, people all around but unseen—though how Wyllea had heard them he had no clue—and an assassin standing before him. It came together to tell him that at least fifteen assassins, if he guessed correctly from the size of the camp below, were hidden around them. So very, very not good.

"Are you deserters?" the man demanded. "The front lines are far to the west."

"My companion and I fell ill as our troop marched to the front. We rested in a village for several days then followed as best we could. Though I fear we may be a little lost in these hills." Wyllea's lie sure sounded convincing.

The man glared.

"That bow is not standard issue. Let me see it." He began striding toward them.

He died with an arrow in his neck before he'd taken three paces. Wyllea's shot had been so fast even the assassin with his preternatural awareness and speed seemed surprised as he died.

So much for talking their way out of this.

Then there were men all around them, charging in with unimaginable speed, and Tirol had no more time to think about anything but staying alive. He managed to draw his sword before the first man reached him, but even as his blade met the other man's, he knew with a certainty that he was no match for such a warrior.

He was a dead man.

CHAPTER 9

*W*yllea had seen The Blacklord's assassins fight before, but she had never faced one herself, let alone twenty of them. She'd always been fast with her bow, faster than any other archer she knew. She drew three arrows from her quiver and fired them in quick succession, taking down three more men, but still she wasn't fast enough. More men would reach her before she could draw and fire again.

She could see Tirol with his blade out, but his fight was going poorly. He was nowhere near fast enough to face such a foe.

Bond with me, now!

This is not the time.

Yes, it is. You'll be faster, stronger, like nothing you have ever known. Bond with me. It's the only way you and he can survive this.

I... She couldn't see any way to win this fight. The

enemy was fast, strong, tough, and there were simply too many of them... *what do I need to do?*

Just give me permission. Let down your guard. I'll do the rest.

Wyllea wasn't sure how to do that, but she did her best. Despite the heat of battle and the men who were mere seconds away from reaching her, she let herself relax, tried to open her mind and body, and hoped to Reisha that she wasn't actually crazy and about to die without a fight.

No, you won't.

The voice filled her louder than ever before as she felt a great force swell inside her. Eaglewing had been right. It was like nothing she'd ever felt before. She felt her muscles tense and swell, her energy increased a hundred-fold. All her senses sharpened, and yet with all the sensations at once she was not overwhelmed. Eaglewing was no longer just a voice in her mind but a full presence, a being that shared her existence. She could feel Eaglewing's elation at the bonding, but the feeling was short-lived, for precious moments were slipping away and she needed to act.

Now it was her own speed that alarmed her. Wyllea was no longer in control. Eaglewing was, and she moved as lightning yet somehow still smooth and easy as a leaping dear.

Another three arrows were out and fired before Wyllea even registered the movement, one of them taking down the man attacking Tirol.

Wyllea leapt and spun like some leaf caught on the wind, spiraling into the air to impossible heights, arrows peppering the black-clad men around her. One threw a knife at her, and it was easily knocked aside by Eaglewing.

She landed lightly, blocking a sword with her bow while simultaneously firing an arrow at that attacker, sending him staggering back with an arrow buried in his belly.

A knife pierced her leg, and at the same time, she saw Tirol tackled by one of the few remaining attackers.

I am sorry, Wyllea, but I need more!

And with that, her entire existence blurred, shifted, collapsed. She could no longer keep track of the fight, the pain, or anything else as the overpowering presence of Eaglewing dominated her. Slowly everything faded to black, and she knew no more.

~

*S*he woke slowly.

Someone was calling her name. What was her name again?

"Wyllea!"

No, her name was Eaglewing. Wasn't it? Everything was hazy.

"Wyllea, please!" She was being shaken.

Eyes fluttered open... her eyes? Yes, but who was she...?

"Oh, thank all the gods. I thought I'd lost you." Tirol was above her, looking down. He looked like crap, his face bruised and bloody, with a nasty gash above his right eye and his hair matted with sweat and blood.

"You don't look so good," she croaked, her voice hoarse and rough. "I don't sound so good."

He smiled, then suddenly leaned in and kissed her.

Ick. This from the part of her that was now Eaglewing.

Yet the part of her that was still Wyllea felt the intensity, the passion, the dire need of the moment, and responded, pressing back, opening her lips to him in a long, lingering kiss. She reached up and grabbed the back of his head to press him closer, but he groaned, wincing, and jerked away.

He sat back, rubbing his head. His eyes seemed a little glassy, and his words were slurred when he said, "Perhaps now isn't the best time." Then his eyes rolled up and he fell over next to her.

She sat up slowly. She who? She was Eaglewing... no, Wyllea. Why was this so difficult? A person should really know who they are, shouldn't they?

I'm sorry, Wyllea. I didn't mean to do that. Well, that's not true. I did mean to do it. I had to in order to win the fight, but, well, I'm sorry I had to do that. This voice was a part of her now as was any limb or organ, ingrained, meshed with her own soul.

Eaglewing? Yes, that is what that part of her was called, her bow but now so much more. So this is what it meant to be "bonded."

Well, yes, sort of. You have to understand I really didn't know how this would work. You aren't a scion, not a Guardian, but I've been with your bloodline for so long now I had thought, had hoped, we would be able to bond and I would have a Guardian once more.

Now Wyllea knew what Eaglewing knew. Guardians of Aehryn and scions, these she understood. Even this talk of Eaglewing being with her bloodline for so long. Everything made sense because she shared one mind with her bow. She had an innate understanding of how this worked.

Eaglewing had had a Guardian long ago, but that bloodline had died off. Yet Eaglewing was an exceptional bow and had been found by Wyllea's great-great-great-grandfather long ago and had stayed with her family since then. It seemed that because Eaglewing had been with only one bloodline for so long that now she'd been able to finally bond with one of that bloodline as she had been bonded, long ago, to her Guardian. Though how this was possible Eaglewing didn't know, and learning more could wait for now.

Wyllea looked over to Tirol, unconscious but still breathing, next to her. She didn't need to ask if Eaglewing could heal him. She already knew she couldn't. Healing was not among her powers.

So is there anything we can do for him?

Perhaps. I can soothe his pain, at least. And you know how to dress a wound. We should be able to patch him up together.

Patch us up too. We took a few hits.

Yes, I know. I can feel your pain. We should dress our leg first. That's the most serious. The rest can wait.

They patched up wounds as best they could. Wyllea's leg had a nasty gash, and she'd lost a lot of blood, but once it was sewn shut and bandaged, it was manageable—painful, but manageable. Eaglewing had powers over the mind and helped her cope with pain.

Next, they tended to Tirol, bandaging his head and tending to the myriad wounds he'd taken. He was lucky to be alive. A survivor for sure, even if he wasn't much good in a fight.

Once he was tended, she wrapped the remainder of her own wounds, all light, then set about searching the bodies of the assassins for anything useful.

Other than weapons, some poisons, and a bit of gold, there wasn't much until she came to the first one she had taken down, probably their leader. He had several pouches filled with various herbs and vials.

Eaglewing had some knowledge of herb lore, and Wyllea unstoppered each vial, sniffing carefully to see if Eaglewing would identify it.

Oh! Eaglewing seemed excited at one in particular. *That one. I know that. It smells of water-based magic. I'd be willing to guess it's a healing potion, very rare, but potent. Try it.*

Are you sure?

Would I put you in danger? I know it well enough. Drink it, but not all, just a sip.

If you say so.

Wyllea tipped the vial to her lips and drank a small portion.

Instantly she was filled with a great sense of warmth and strength. Her aches and pains disappeared, even the pain of her leg, which Eaglewing was suppressing, seemed to vanish.

Curious, Wyllea stoppered the vial, then checked her

wound. It was closed and no longer weeping, her stitches expelled from the newly reformed flesh.

"That's impressive."

See. I told you.

Can someone who isn't conscious drink it?

No. But once Tirol wakes, we can give him some. He'll need more, maybe half what's left. Quite useful.

I'll say.

Wyllea finished her scrounging then made a quick camp, assembling a fire and having some of her food. She was famished. Apparently, bonding, fighting off a score of magically enhanced assassins, then healing yourself took a lot out of you.

When Tirol woke near dusk, she gave him some of the healing potion, and he instantly perked up.

"What is that?"

"Healing potion."

"Where did you get that?"

"Off one of the Assassins. I didn't think he'd need it anymore."

Tirol gave a short laugh. After a moment of checking his wounds and discarding blood-soaked bandages which were no longer needed, he sat next to her by the fire.

"I really didn't think we were going to win that. I'm still not sure how we did, though I seem to recall you spinning into the air, shooting arrows so fast a dozen men dropped. What happened?"

"I'm not sure I can fully explain it myself. But I now know my bow is, well, quite magical and powerful."

"Your bow?"

"Her name is Eaglewing."

"Your bow has a name?" The incredulity was clear on his face even in the dying light of day.

Wyllea grimaced. "I told you it was hard to explain."

He nodded. "Well, I'm just happy to be alive."

She gave a short laugh. "Yes, I know. You were quite... passionate about that fact when you woke me."

"You remember that?"

"I do."

"And..." He drew a breath, hesitant. "How did you feel about it?"

She was about to say that she felt a certain intensity to the moment as well, but Eaglewing interrupted.

Senia is close. They've stopped for the night not far from here. If we leave now, we can get to them by midnight.

Understood.

She couldn't remember what she had been about to say to Tirol and shrugged it off. "We need to leave."

"What? Why?"

"Remember that whole 'magical bow' thing? Well, it also has a mind of its own, and right now it's sensing someone in distress. We need to help. I'm sorry to drag you along on this, but Eaglewing is... very persuasive. I'm going. Are you coming?"

He nodded. "Of course, I would... that is, yes."

They gathered up their things and left, heading north and west as Eaglewing directed.

CHAPTER 10

Tirol was more confused than ever.

He'd asked a direct question, and she'd evaded it. It was fairly obvious now she didn't feel as he did. He'd thought in that last moment of the kiss, when she had reached to press him closer, that she'd wanted him. Perhaps she'd just been caught up in the moment. And that was before he'd pulled away and fainted. How very manly of him. Could a warrior like her be with a man like him? He didn't know, and it seemed she wasn't going to tell him.

Instead, they were off on some strange quest to save... someone?

He flirted with the thought that perhaps she wasn't all there. Her mind was going. But then... she'd defeated a host of assassins pretty much on her own. He hadn't killed even one. To do that, with the power the assassins possessed, must have taken some powerful magic on her part. So perhaps...

Again, he didn't really know, and she wasn't saying much more on the topic.

Gods, but she could be infuriating!

They'd been moving through the night at a fast pace, Wyllea pointing out divots, roots, or other obstacles in the darkness which he would have missed. Her night vision was definitely exceptional.

"We're getting close," she whispered and slowed the pace, creeping through some dense brush in a narrow valley.

Triol could see a flickering light in the distance through the bushes, someone's fire.

Well, they were certainly heading somewhere.

As they drew near, he could make out figures in the clearing. She turned to him and whispered close to his ear, her hot breath sending a not-unpleasant tingling through him and warming him in ways he'd rather not say.

"Stay here. I'll see what I can do, but Eaglewing says the man up ahead is very dangerous." The message was clear. Tirol would be a liability and not someone to have around when things got dangerous. He nodded, hiding his anger and frustration. He wasn't upset that she was leaving him behind. The gods knew he wouldn't be much help to her. He more was irritated at himself for not being much help.

She smiled and moved away, silent as the night wind.

He adjusted his position slightly to get a better view of the clearing through the dense brush and watched. His ears grew accustomed to the quiet of the night after a moment, and he could hear those before him.

A man crossed his line of sight on the other side of their small fire. It was only briefly, but he made out a tall, broad frame, well built and strong. He was dressed in black leather armor with a large sword on his back. His hair was dark, and the man turned slightly such that Tirol caught a glimpse of his eyes. No light shone in those menacing orbs.

The man was talking to someone Tirol couldn't see.

"... first thing in the morning, so you might as well sleep. You know you can't escape. You're nothing without your sword."

The voice that responded was female, high and light. "I'll find a way to escape. Either that or Ahrn will come for me."

"Yes, your pathetic man. He's no match for me, and you know it. He's a normal man, even if he is an exceptional warrior. I defeated you with ease. He'll be no issue at all.

"You won't win," was the woman's defiant response.

The man laughed.

His laughing stopped abruptly. His eyes darted to the side. In the next instant, his hand came up with incredible speed, a blur. In his clenched fist, he held an arrow, the metal point just pricking his neck and drawing a bead of blood.

"I think that's the closest anyone has ever come to hitting me," he said evenly. Then he was moving again, so fast, rolling away from another arrow and coming up with his sword in hand.

"Show yourself," he called into the night. Tirol could almost detect a hint of fear in his voice. The man's sword twitched, knocking another arrow away from hitting him. A flurry of arrows hailed down on him, and every one of them was swept away by the black, light-sucking blade of the warrior's sword.

Wyllea must have been getting frustrated by now. Something moved across Tirol's vision and a moment later the woman from the clearing was throwing herself bodily at the man. He easily stepped out of the way, knocking another arrow from the air.

He laughed. "Do you really think you can best me?" With his next breath, he launched himself into the night. A moment later there was a commotion from the brush where Tirol guessed Wyllea had been hiding.

Wyllea came tumbling out of the brush, coming up firing arrows at the man who strode out behind her, easily swatting away her attacks.

"By the gods, what are you?" Wyllea cried, exasperated.

"The luckiest man alive," he said, grinning. "I don't know how another scion found me, but now I have two of you to take back to my master."

"What are you talking about?"

With another burst of incredible speed, the man advanced on her. She blocked his strike with her bow, but only just. He attacked with a flash of the dark blade, swiping over and over again. She blocked again and again, but Tirol could see her movements were not as fast as the man's, not as smooth.

With a twist and slash, Wyllea's bow was pulled from her hands and tossed to the far side of the small clearing. The other woman dove for the weapon, but the man was faster, gripping Wyllea, pulling her up in front of him, and raising his sword to her neck. "Touch it and she dies."

The other woman froze, frustration and anger playing on a young face with brilliant blue eyes and amber hair that fell like a curtain across her features. She rose slowly, defiance written in every movement and look.

The man laughed again, knowing he'd won.

"Come over here, Senia," he said, smug arrogance clear in his voice. The other woman moved stiffly, the grim determination and resistance on her face turning to resigned frustration.

"I'm sorry," she said to Wyllea.

When the other woman, Senia, was far enough away from Wyllea's bow, the man withdrew his sword from Wyllea's neck, only to then bring the pommel down swiftly on the back of her head with a wet crack. Wyllea dropped to the ground, limp, and the man took two long strides to meet Senia.

"It's too bad I only have one of these," he said grabbing the strange-looking bindings Senia wore on her wrists. "But it will have to do." He withdrew a leather thong from around his neck from which hung a golden key. He pulled the thong over his head and proceeded to unlock one side of the bindings on Senia. Once that side was off, he rotated the bindings around the one hand they were still attached to, and with a command to "kneel," he forced Senia to the ground. There he affixed the open side to one of Wyllea's wrists, locked it, and put the thong with the key back around his neck.

The man then laid his hand on the back of Wyllea's

head and a dark nimbus surrounded him for the briefest of moments. Tirol wasn't sure what had happened, but his gut told him the man had used magic, though to do what, he didn't know.

The man turned to Senia before he rose, his face near to hers with a conceited grin. "I hope you see now, you have no chance of escape. Not even another scion could save you."

She punched him. Her one hand, now free from the bindings, landed a solid strike to his jaw, turning his head slightly. It hardly seemed to faze him. Tirol could see blue fire burning in Senia's eyes, but the man just laughed again as he stood.

"Get some sleep. We still have a long distance to go to see my master."

Tirol sat back on his haunches for a moment, still not fully able to believe that Wyllea had been subdued and captured. It hadn't been easy for the man, but it had hardly taken more than a few moments and the woman Tirol thought to be invincible was lying unconscious in the clearing before him.

The truly sad part was there was nothing he could do to help her. If she couldn't defeat this man, there was no way Tirol had any chance. Tirol even contemplated simply running away. He was useless here.

That was when the true war started inside him.

Running was the smart move. It was the one that would keep him alive. He wasn't a hero. He was a survivor. His father had been the hero and had died for a cause. Tirol had sworn he would never be that stupid. Yet his mind countered with the fact that his father has left those he loved behind, something Tirol wasn't going to do. He wouldn't leave. He couldn't leave. His mind kept working around the problem of how to free Wyllea despite its futility.

His self-preservation side kept trying to convince him to go. It replayed the fight he'd just seen over and over and with a certainty told him staying was death. If he wanted to live another day, he would go and forget about this stupid woman with her intoxicating energy and brilliant green eyes.

To stay was death. So he turned, ready to go.

But to stay meant remaining with Wyllea. He turned back.

To go was to live. Perhaps, if he lived, he could rescue her later. He turned away again.

But he knew deep down that now would be his best chance. He didn't think a man bogged down with two prisoners would move that fast, so perhaps Tirol could keep pace with them, watch for an opening. Yet this was no ordinary man, and most likely Tirol wouldn't be able to keep up. He didn't know how he knew that, but the uncertainty of whether or not he might ever get another chance to save Wyllea caused him to turn back once again.

He warred with himself into the night.

Ultimately, his self-preservation side asked the question he had hoped to avoid: *Why?*

The question rang through him: *Why do this for her? Why stay?*

The answer, though he knew it in his soul, took him no small amount of time to admit.

Because he loved her.

In that moment, everything fell into place for him.

He was willing to sacrifice himself for her because he loved her. His father had left his family not for some greater cause but to fight *for* his family, to protect them because he loved them. Perhaps it wasn't foolish to sacrifice yourself if it's for those you love.

Now sure, resolute, he stood again, peering into the clearing. The fire was reduced to a lick of flame on glowing embers. It was quiet. The dangerous man was sleeping.

Suddenly a plan hatched in Tirol's mind. He could help Wyllea and the other woman escape, though they would still be bound. Something told him, however, that no mere smith would be able to break the bonds that held these two women. That meant that the only way to free Wyllea was to remove the bonds, and that meant getting the key from the dark warrior's neck. The man slept, so it should be easy, but Tirol's gut told him not to believe that assumption. The man might have some ward that would wake him, or he might just be a light sleeper. No, there was a surefire way to guarantee the man didn't wake up. If Tirol was worried about magic, well, he happened to have a little magic of his own to counter it.

He took out his pouch of sleeping powder. He only had a little left, perhaps just more than one dose, which for a big man like that would probably do just fine. He had to get close enough to use it though. Luckily, he'd always been quiet, and his years as a thief had honed those skills to a fine edge.

He moved carefully through the brush and the darkness. It was torturously slow going to ensure he made no sound in the thick brush, but he knew he had the time and even one misstep could cause him his life.

Eventually, he crept out into the clearing, moving with a steady pace, measuring each stride and placing each foot with care. It felt like hours before he finally knelt next to the big man. He took the pouch of sleeping powder and simply upended it over the man's head, letting the fine dust drift down to be inhaled and take effect.

Nothing happened, but that was a good sign. The man was still sleeping, hopefully much more deeply now. Triol moved carefully, slowly, not wishing to tempt fate as he pulled the thong with the key up out of the man's shirt. He drew out his knife, cut through the leather thong, and slipped the key off.

Tirol smiled. He'd done it!

A hand grabbed his wrist. The grip was like steel shackles, immovable. The man's eyes were trying to open as his mouth formed slurred words.

"Who... are... you...?" the man said, eyes just barely breaking open, head lifted slightly. Then they sagged closed again and he fell back. The grip on Tirol's arm loosened.

Tirol tried to pull away, but the grip returned a moment later, the man's eyes opening again.

"What've you... done?" Came the thick voice, the words barely distinguishable. "Why can't I...?" The grip grew tighter. Tirol winced in pain as bones threatened to break. "Who. Are. You?" Each word was forced, almost a yell as the man levered himself onto his elbow.

Gods, but Tirol hated magic! Why did his sleeping dust have to fail this one time!

The man fell back a bit, that last effort seeming a great strain for him. Yet, still he didn't let Tirol go.

Another voice piped up. "Who are you? Are you here to help us?"

Tirol looked to see the other woman, Senia, awake.

He smiled. "Yes." And he tossed her the key. It landed in her lap, a perfect throw. "Free yourself and Wyllea, then get the hell out of here, before this maniac is fully awake!" He didn't quite know until the words had come out exactly what they meant. But as he heard them, they just felt right. Yes, he might die—well almost certainly would die—but as long as Wyllea escaped, he'd be at peace with that choice.

Senia started on the bindings with the key.

The hand on his wrist tightened. Tirol turned back to the man, gritting his teeth as his muscle and flesh compressed. Tears came to his eyes, so intense was the pain. The man's hand tightened, crushing bone, demolishing Tirol's wrist and hand. Tirol screamed, a desperate howl of pain even to his own ears. He couldn't think, couldn't move. It felt like his hand was made solely of sharp, biting pain.

"What is this?" the man next to him bellowed and started to rise, bringing Tirol with him. The man got to his feet, still unsteady, jerking Tirol to stand with him. The man's other hand caught Tirol's neck just under his jaw, forcing Tirol's face upward to meet the large man's gaze. "Who do you think you are, little man? Coming into my camp and..."

"Emberthorn!" Senia called, and in the dark of the night a blue light erupted from somewhere behind him.

The man before him cursed, glaring at Tirol. "This is your fault!" With that, the man released his wrist, and the hand at his neck squeezed, lifting him off his feet like he was nothing at all, then tossed him like a rag. Tirol gasped for air, his breath not coming as he flew through the air. Then his head hit something hard. He was aware only long enough to feel his body collapse to the ground in a heap before darkness took him.

CHAPTER 11

*W*yllea came awake as someone shook her.

The woman next to her had undone their bindings and was saying something. "Quickly, call your bow, we only have..."

"What's this?" the dark warrior bellowed from across the clearing, drawing Wyllea's attention away.

The man had Tirol!

He stood, unsteady, heaving Tirol up with him. He grabbed Tirol's throat and said, "Who do you think you are, little man? Coming into my camp and..."

Then the woman next to her stood in one quick motion, saying, "Emberthorn!" In that instant a massive sword appeared in her hands, a great blue flame coming to life on its blade.

Call my name! Eaglewing sent to her.

Yet before she could, the man said something to Tirol then tossed him into the night like a doll. Tirol tumbled through the air, slammed into a tree trunk at the edge of the clearing, and crashed, limp, to the ground.

Things were happening too fast.

The other man drew his sword, its shadowed blade hard to see in the night, and strode toward them. Senia stood proud and ready, a grim smile on her face.

Call me!

Right! Sorry.

"Eaglewing!" And there was the bow in her hand. But she had no arrows.

You need no ammunition now that we're bonded, simply draw the string as if you had an arrow, and one will appear.

Oh!

She did so, and an arrow of green light formed, ready to fire. She fired.

The man knocked it away with his sword as he drew closer, though this time, he seemed to twitch and wince when he did.

This is useless!

No, it's not. You must keep trying. Though I've never sensed anyone like this man before, he won't be able to evade your shots forever. He'll make a mistake, they all do.

He didn't the last time.

He wasn't fighting another scion at the same time the last time.

True, but there is something I have to do first.

The dark warrior was upon them. His blade met the other woman's. So began a fight of such fury and speed that even with her advanced senses it was only just possible for Wyllea to follow each move. They seemed to be fairly evenly matched, and since she had other concerns at the moment, she let them fight. She did fire off three quick arrows just to distract the large man, but he deflected them without even changing his pattern of moves against Senia, smooth and easy. Gods, but he was good.

Wyllea dashed into the brush, trying to remember where she'd left her pack.

What about the fight? Eaglewing asked. She didn't need to ask Wyllea what she was doing, both were very aware of the plan.

She's fine for the moment, and Tirol's life is more important.

True.

With Eaglewing's enhanced night sight, she located it quick enough and scrounged inside until she found the small vial she was looking for. Then she raced back to the clearing.

She spared a glance to see how the woman was doing. She was holding her own. At this point, it seemed neither of the two had the upper hand. That said, the man still seemed to be slightly groggy and only just getting up to speed. Wyllea had the suspicion that if she didn't help soon he would quickly get the upper hand.

She went to Tirol and knelt next to him. He didn't look good. His one hand was a bruised mess, bleeding from several places where bone had broken skin. His throat was similarly bruised and his breathing forced. Then there was his head where he'd hit the tree. A large open gash across his forehead poured blood across one-half of his face.

Wyllea slapped him, hard, and with her enhanced

strength from Eaglewing, it would have been a significant blow.

He woke, eyes wide then quickly going glassy, but it was enough. He was conscious, and she popped the stopper on the vial and poured all of what remained down his throat. He drank. The wound on his forehead puckered and closed. The bruises at his throat and wrist disappeared, and the wrist filled out from its crushed state, closing all open wounds.

Tirol blinked, wiped blood from his face, then looked at her.

"I told the other woman to get you out of here."

Wyllea shook her head. "I wouldn't leave you."

"Oh." He smiled. "Wyllea, I..."

"Not now. We have a fight to win." She rose and motioned to the other two.

"Ah, right. Well, you go. I'll just sit here and collect myself for a moment."

She nodded and turned to the combat.

"You didn't defeat me last time, and you won't this time, give up Senia!" the man said derisively.

It hadn't even been that long, but it seemed as if he was starting to gain the upper hand, attacking more than defending. Wyllea crept quietly until she was directly behind him then unleashed the full fury of Eaglewing's wrath upon the man.

The shadow sword was there, lifted high, blade down behind his back to block the first arrow, then he leapt to the side. Wyllea saw her mistake instantly, for the other woman... Senia, who'd not seen the arrows coming was now directly in their path. Yet the other woman's speed and grace were amazing, and she blocked two before the rest of the arrows simply vanished.

You can make them go away?

I can. Interesting trick, isn't it?

I'll say.

Then Wyllea fired volley after volley at the man, who danced and jumped around the clearing to evade the attacks from both women. He even began to laugh at one point.

"Now this is a fight!" he yelled into the night, beating aside another arrow, then deftly blocking a strike from Senia.

Then it happened.

He got too cocky. In her next attack, Senia's sequence of blows caused him to step back, but he was already at the edge of the clearing. His foot caught a tree root, and he misstepped. Wyllea fired, and even though he still tried to dodge the attack, it caught him with a long, glancing blow across his ribs, ripping through his armor.

He beat back Senia and leapt away again, but when he landed, Wyllea had already fired. He deflected the arrow, but not well enough, and it slashed across his thigh.

The man turned, leaping away... or at least he would have.

But the one person forgotten in this melee stopped him.

Tirol's short sword slid into the man's belly. The large man clutched at it, staggering back. Tirol lost his grip on the weapon but quickly had a dagger out and pounced, sinking the weapon into the man's shoulder. The man fell with Tirol atop him.

The man had enough strength to try to lift his sword to attack Tirol, but Senia was there, knocking the blade down and away, then kicking it out of his hand and bringing her burning blade, Emberthorn, to the man's throat.

Tirol plucked out his dagger and drew back, meaning to strike again, but Senia called out, "Stop!"

Tirol froze. "I'll kill him," he said through clenched teeth.

"No, you won't." Senia, though still young by all appearances, had a very commanding voice, and Tirol didn't move. He didn't put his dagger away, but he also didn't attack. He sat rigid, ready to strike.

"Give me one good reason why?"

"Because he's The Blacklord's son, and I have so very many questions to ask him." With that, she knelt next to the man and slammed her sword down on his head. The blow probably would have killed any normal man, but this one just went limp, still breathing.

"The Blacklord has a son?" Tirol said, lowering his dagger, his words echoing Wyllea's own thoughts.

"He does, and he may hold the key to winning the war."

~

Wyllea sat next to the fire, feeling all the aches of the past day, physical and emotional, come back to her.

The past few hours had seen some amazing highs and some devastating lows and had pushed her to her limits physically. She was exhausted, body and soul. If it wasn't for the extra energy and vigor obtained through her connection with Eaglewing, she'd be fast asleep.

She didn't feel quite so bad about being defeated by the one Senia called Davar, or the Dark Scion, knowing now how tough he was. He'd had a sword clean through his gut, but as soon as they had removed it, the wound had started healing. As it was, with not much time having passed, the moon still unset in the sky, he was nearly fully healed. Luckily, he was still unconscious. They had put his own special manacles on him. Senia said the restraints would keep him from contacting or using his scion sword. This is what he'd used on Senia to get her this far. They had also bound him to a stout tree, though given his immense strength Wyllea wondered how much that might stop him. Senia seemed to think that without his sword he'd be far weaker. That remained to be seen. Senia had also placed something called a "spirit ward" on him so they would know when he awoke. It seemed a lot, but this man was The Blacklord's son.

The Blacklord's son.

The most powerful man in the world had a son. A man so powerful in magic he'd sustained his own life for over two hundred years, and this was his offspring? No wonder Davar was no easy foe to best. And to think he'd been brought low by Tirol.

That brought her mind to the jumbled mess of emotions and thoughts that surrounded the spry hunter.

He was fast asleep next to the fire. She was sure he was exhausted as well and didn't have the benefit of a magical item to keep him awake. On one hand, she couldn't figure out why he was still with her. She'd forced him into several situations she was sure he would have run far and fast from otherwise. He'd seemed somewhat taken with her back at the creek... had that been only yesterday? Yet she couldn't imagine anyone being so smitten with her that they'd follow her through all of this. She wasn't anything special, an average woman and a warrior. For most men, the warrior part scared them away. And yet, on the other hand, she really couldn't imagine life without him anymore. It was the oddest thing. He'd been in her life only a few days, less than a full week, and she found his company... reassuring, steady, enjoyable. She wanted to have him around, but couldn't truly understand what it was that made him stay.

She'd been terrified that Tirol hadn't survived Davar's attack. She'd seen more than enough men die around her in her years in the army. But if he died, that would be... different, and she didn't know why.

Gods, but you humans are a mess, Eaglewing said.

I won't argue with you on that point.

Do you really not understand your own feelings?

Right now, there's little I understand. Why? Do you understand any of this?

I've been with a few bonded humans in my time. I know enough.

So why do I feel this way?

In my experience, you'll need to figure that out on your own. My interference really won't do much to help.

Great, thanks.

Anytime. Wyllea could tell Eaglewing was grinning and hated her for it.

"I still can't believe it. Another scion." This from Senia, sitting on the other side of the fire.

"I take it there aren't many?" Wyllea asked.

"I thought I was the only one."

"Oh." Wyllea studied the other woman for a moment. Even though she was young, not past twenty, if Wyllea guessed correctly, she had an air of strength about her. She sat straight, poised, confident, with her head slightly forward such that her long reddish hair fell around her face. In a lot of ways, she was the opposite of Wyllea, tall, slender, young, and beautiful to Wyllea's average height and curvy, weathered exterior. And though Wyllea wouldn't consider herself to be old, she had more than half a decade on the other woman and had led a hard life, seeing things in her years which had made her feel older still.

Yet Wyllea sensed that on the inside the two of them were very similar, strong, assured, confident warriors. Senia deserved the truth.

"I'm not a true scion."

Senia's head came up, her looks curious. "What do you mean?"

Wyllea smiled. "Forgive me. I'm new to this and still don't really fully understand all the details, but from what I understand from Eaglewing, our bonding wasn't normal.

Where you're a descendant of some great warrior from long ago, I'm not."

"But then, how...?"

"I don't rightly know myself, but it seems that Eaglewing here has been in my family for generations. From my own knowledge, I know that this same bow was passed down from my great-great-great-grandfather to me. So according to Eaglewing, since she has been with my bloodline for so long, she started to form a new attachment to us. This attachment had grown strong enough that when my own defenses were weak enough she was able to break through and communicate with me. Once that happened, our connection grew stronger and stronger until I finally let her fully bond with me."

"I wouldn't have thought that possible."

"Well, apparently it is."

"Apparently." Senia was quiet for a moment, then grinned. "I can tell you this. When we get back to St. Antin, there are going to be a lot of people who will want to talk to you and figure out what happened."

"I recall hearing of St. Antin. Last I heard, all of Hallania was retreating to the fortress. Does it still stand?"

"It did five days ago when I was captured. Though without me I don't know how well they fared."

"You certainly have a high opinion of yourself."

Senia smiled. "It's not like that. Emberthorn is tied to the Element of Fire, which in turn represents spirit. One of the more subtle abilities I possess is to lift and inspire the spirits of those around me. That, along with my battle prowess and other enhanced attributes, means that I'm often seen as a beacon of light, of hope, by those around me."

She didn't really know where the knowledge came from, but Wyllea said, "Eaglewing is of Wind and Mind. I'm still figuring out the full extent of her powers, but there's an innate knowing which I seem to have acquired by virtue of the bonding."

Senia nodded her understanding. "The monks at the abbey can help you learn all your abilities and train you to deepen them. You'll make a fine addition to our fight."

Wyllea drew in a long breath and looked over at Tirol's still form. Would he join this fight? He wasn't a warrior, though his skills at stealth and tracking were exceptional. It would be his choice, but there was a part of her that hoped he'd choose to stay and fight, hoped he was the man she so desired him to be.

"What's his story?" Senia asked.

"We met only a few days ago in a town—"

"Davar's awake!" Senia interrupted.

Wyllea turned to see The Blacklord's son still and unmoving where they'd tied him to the tree. He was not far away, a few long paces. She raised Eaglewing and pulled back the string, just to be safe.

A moment later, the man's head rose slowly, a sly smile on his face. He seemed well enough now, all his wounds healed. Senia and Wyllea sat tense, waiting.

"Ladies," he said with a bob of his head. He moved against the ropes binding him, but they held and he grimaced. "Usually I'm not the one tied up, but if you want to take advantage of me, I supposed I could let you."

Wyllea relaxed a little. He seemed fairly secure. Nonetheless, she kept Eaglewing at the ready.

"What do we do now?" she asked Senia.

"Watch him like a hawk," the other woman said with a shrug.

Wyllea had a better idea. She loosed three arrows into him. He grunted in pain as the three mystically created arrows faded away. He didn't even bleed, but he did seem distracted and faint. "Let him heal that."

Senia gave a short, harsh laugh. "Fair enough."

They were both wary now, though, and took turns watching him as the night progressed.

It was a short while later, the moon having set, when something sprang to life at the edge of Wyllea's senses.

She looked over to Senia who was tilting her head as if listening intently.

What is that? She asked Eaglewing, still not having been with the weapon long enough to know all the signs and sensations of their bonding.

Someone—make that many someones—are heading this way fast!

"Someone's coming," she and Senia said over each other as they both rose, weapons ready.

Wyllea spared a moment to nudge Tirol with her toe.

He groaned.

"Wake up. I think another fight is on the way."

"Great," he mumbled, his voice thick. He rose slowly, groaning again.

Then there was no more time to talk as dark forms

dropped into the small clearing. More of The Blacklord's assassins and—

Wyllea blinked. That wasn't possible.

"Hello, ladies," said a man who was a twin to Davar.

She spared a glance at The Blacklord's son. He still sat, still tied to the tree, smiling.

"Who are you?" Senia challenged as everyone in the clearing stood poised, ready. Only Tirol was unprepared, rising to his feet groggily and taking out his sword.

"I would love to stay and chat, but I have to free my... brother." Wyllea noticed the pause and without really thinking sent her senses into the man. One of Eaglewing's powers was to read minds, but her senses found nothing there to read.

Odd.

She didn't have more time to ponder it, however.

"Shadowfang!" the twin called, and Davar's sword appeared in his hands.

Wait... that wasn't right. These weapons were unique and could only be wielded by one person. And why would The Blacklord's sons share a sword? These thoughts would have to wait, as attacks were coming at her from all side, and she sprung into the fight.

She was more used to the feel of Eaglewing now than that first fight with The Blacklord's assassins. She'd been unable to handle the speed, the abilities, and had blacked out, but now, despite a difference of only a few hours, she flowed with Eaglewing into the fray, and the first thing she did was get to higher ground—well... not ground at all.

She leapt into the air, stopping about thirty feet up,

and there she floated. Eaglewing was of wind, and she could fly when needed.

She rained arrows down on those below, but from her raised vantage, she could see other assassins moving through the night, hopping over or slinking through the thick brush below. There must have been fifty in all. Yet between her arrows and Emberthorn's blue-burning blade, they dropped quickly. Her fight with Davar had been so much more challenging than this. That brought her mind to The Blacklord's son and his twin.

The twin was ignoring the fight, guarding his brother and letting his minions keep the scions busy. But why wasn't he attacking?

Davar is doing something with his mind. I can sense it, but I don't know what. Eaglewing was concerned. *He's a powerful wind talent. His mental powers are strong. Not as strong as us, but if his brother is the same, that's probably why we couldn't read him earlier.*

Wyllea looked around, her senses mixed with Eaglewing's. Between shots at the ever-increasing number of assassins heading their way, she tried to figure out what Davar was doing.

I don't need to know what he's doing. She fired several arrows at his head. But that's where the brother came in, deflecting the shots at his twin.

Blazes!

There! I've figured out what he's up to. It was such a fine usage of wind it took me a moment.

I don't need to know the details. Just show me!

There! Eaglewing couldn't point, but Wyllea knew where to look. There was a pouch tied tightly on Senia's belt. The drawstring had been pulled open carefully. Senia hadn't even noticed. Then a brief gust of wind blew into the pouch, inflating it and blowing out its contents, a golden key.

"Senia!" But even as Wyllea shouted the name, the key flew like a shot to the hand of Davar's twin. "He's got the key. He'll be free in a moment!"

Senia spun, clapping a hand over the pouch, feeling its emptiness. She swore.

"I can't leave," was the reply.

Wyllea could see why. Senia couldn't move far from her spot without exposing Tirol to attack. As quick and agile as the man was, he simply wasn't up to fighting the assassins, even just one on one, after everything he'd been through today. He could keep from taking a hit but probably wouldn't get any chance to strike, meaning it was a fight of exhaustion and he was already tired.

"Go. I'll protect him," Wyllea called and focused her shots on those around Tirol. Her magical arrows fell with the speed and deadly force of lightning, flashing through the night.

Senia fought the twin, though Wyllea had no idea how the young woman would fare against two of them. But once Davar had freed himself from the bindings, he leapt away, disappearing in a puff of shadow-smoke.

A moment later, the second one did the same, letting the sword fall, but before it even hit the ground, it too vanished into wisps of shadow.

Within a few heartbeats, the remaining assassins were dealt with. Wyllea landed, floating to the ground.

Her mind was whirling about Davar and his twin, but her first thought was for Tirol.

"Are you hurt?" she asked him, surprising herself at the concern and worry in her voice.

He smiled, looking tired and worn like he'd been fighting for hours as opposed to only scant minutes. "No. You kept them off me." Then he sat heavily and sighed. "But I really need a long nap."

Wyllea turned to Senia

"That was odd."

Senia nodded. "Why didn't they attack when they had the chance? Two of them against me would probably not have gone well."

Thoughts finally started clicking into place for Wyllea. "I don't think there were two of them." She raised a hand to forestall the question she saw on Senia's lips. "Hear me out. His talent with mind is strong, but mine is stronger. When I probed the twin, I felt nothing. It wasn't a barrier. It was just... nothing. There was no mind there. I think the twin was some sort of construct or illusion. Also, if they really were brothers, both sons of The Blacklord, why would they share one sword? The twin should have had his own, but instead he used Davar's. I think it was some form of defensive ability, a duplicate to throw people off."

Senia was nodding. "That makes sense." She sighed heavily. "But he's gone now." She cocked her head to one side. "My hearing is exceptional, but I can't hear him at all."

"I'm sorry. I..." Wyllea had been about to say she couldn't sense him either, but... no.

Is that him? She asked Eaglewing.

Yes. You were close to him long enough for me to get a good strong sense of his mind. He is heading east fast.

Can we catch him?

Of course we can.

Then let's.

"I know where he is. I'll get him back." With that, she sprung into the air, the night wind howling around her as she flew with amazing speed toward where Davar bounded along, heading east. He moved in a strange combination of running and leaping, his jumps carrying him for miles at a time over forests and rivers or other obstacles.

It took only scant moments for her to catch up, flying free with amazing speed above everything. There remained only one problem when she found him.

I can't see him. She'd learned that her eyesight had become much more than exceptional when she'd bonded with Eaglewing. Like an eagle herself, she could see minute items at great distances, but even though she could sense Davar's mind below, she couldn't see him.

She suspected with a sword named Shadowfang, his ability to become shadow itself and hide in the night was also exceptional.

But she could still sense him, or his mind at least, and that was her advantage.

She drew back Eaglewing's string and, letting her mind's eye guide the shot, loosed an arrow.

He easily moved out of the way. Yet when he next hit the ground, he stopped. She flew past him, then circled around, returning to where he stood in a wide field. She approached carefully. He had revealed himself, shadows no longer cloaking him. He stood ready, sword held easily in one hand. She floated down until she was hovering twenty feet from him, still well off the ground.

"I didn't think either of you would be stupid enough to follow me," he said with a confident grin. He had lots of reasons to be confident. He'd been stabbed in the gut earlier that night as well as shot by her three arrows and was now perfectly fine.

Wyllea said nothing, trying to figure out how to win this fight. Just shooting arrows at him might score a hit eventually, emphasis on *might* and *eventually*. Even then, he could heal incredibly fast. She couldn't. She had the advantage of a ranged weapon and greater speed if he chose to flee again, but other than that, she was at a loss.

"What are you waiting for?" he asked, still confident, but she could hear the confusion in his voice. Apparently, he wasn't used to his opponent being so careful.

He shrugged. "Let's end this." He leapt at her.

She flew back and away, the wind that was hers to command blowing her out of his reach. His leap took him hundreds of feet into the air, a slash with his sword brushing less than a foot away from her, but that was all. He landed, and once again, she joined him, hovering, ready.

"Why won't you fight me?" he shouted, angry. Perhaps she could use that anger.

"Like I'm going to make this easy for you," she said evenly. "I know you wish to capture me, and you know I wish to capture you. Our abilities are matched. We are in a stalemate."

"We are hardly a match." He leapt again.

This time she didn't move, she blocked his blow with Eaglewing turning the blade to the side and grabbing his wrist, and then she flew downward fast. She landed and slammed him into the ground in front of her. She released him and fired as fast as she could, but he rolled out of the way and spun to his feet. She leapt backward into the air, but he followed. She fired a stream of arrows, all of which he knocked aside. When he swung at her, she pushed herself farther away with a gust of wind and again his blade sliced too near for comfort. She fired at the same time as his swing. He flinched away, the arrow catching him in the shoulder as opposed to the neck. He landed, and she kept her distance.

She fired at him, but even with a wounded shoulder, he blocked her shots.

I need something else. Arrows just aren't going to do it. What else can we do to him? She asked Eaglewing.

His mind is strong. I've already assessed that. Getting through his defenses will take some work, but we are stronger. We can do it if we have a little time.

Let's do it. She didn't need to ask how. She knew what Eaglewing knew for the most part.

It was odd working in the metaphysical realm, attacking with her mind. She and Eaglewing could attack the mind directly, a mental blast that would stagger and disorient, possibly even knock unconscious. It helped if she thought of the attacks as some giant invisible hammer pounding down on the person's head.

They struck. He blinked.

"Is that all you've got?" he said with a sneer.

Far from it. That was just one blow.

She began hammering down on him, strike after strike. It didn't matter if he moved, it was a mental attack, and as long as she could sense his mind, it was at risk.

She could sense his defenses weakening.

"No!" he cried out and leapt at her again.

Keep it up, Wyllea said to Eaglewing as she fired one arrow after another and flew backward to evade his blow. Eaglewing kept attacking his mind and, halfway through his leap, he fell from the sky with a shriek.

He disappeared before he landed, shadow cloaking him invisible in the night, but his mind was not hidden.

His defenses were breaking, crumbling, which was good because the repeated attacks were starting to drain her.

She landed next to where he had fallen, a ball of black on a darkened field.

The darkness lunged at her, shrouded her in shadow, but she knew where he was, knew his mind. She was in now. Even though she could not see it, she blocked a blow from his sword, knowing where he'd placed it, seeing the thought behind the stroke. Then she fired five quick shots into him. With his mind weakened, he managed to dodge only three. One hit his stomach, the other his sword arm.

He cried out, going to one knee.

One final hammer to his mind as she peppered him with a barrage of arrows, and he crumbled. All but one arrow hit home. His mind reeled.

One final blow and his shadows faded from around them as he fell into a darkness of his own, unconscious.

Wyllea breathed hard, her head aching.

I've never hit anyone with that many mind bolts before. That was intense! Eaglewing sounded winded and worn.

I know. I can feel it too.

For the sake of certainty, she fired another barrage of arrows into him. She knew he would heal, and he seemed far from dead, just out cold.

Senia dropped out of the sky.

She looked at the limp form of Davar filled with arrows. Surprised and laughing, she said, "I didn't think I was that far behind you. What did you do?"

"Remembered I could do more than just hit people with arrows. I'm still not quite used to this 'being a Guardian with strange powers' thing."

Senia chuckled again. "I know what that feels like. That was me not that long ago." She nodded to Davar. "Shall we take him in?"

Wyllea nodded. "I'm beat, but let's get him back into the bindings at least. I'd also suggest keeping him unconscious for as long as we can."

"I agree. Can you do that with your mind powers?"

"Yes, for now. I'll let you know if I get too tired."

"Do that."

When they returned to the camp where they had left Tirol, they found him sleeping soundly. Wyllea pounded a couple more mental blasts into Davar's mind, then collapsed herself, exhausted.

"You up for keeping watch?" she asked Senia, who nodded. "Good." She laid herself next to Tirol and joined him in slumber.

CHAPTER 12

Tirol was quite certain he didn't like flying. Especially when all that kept him from falling was Wyllea's arms around him. Not that he minded her arms around him or the feel of her body pressed against his. Those were quite pleasant sensations. They were, however, harder to enjoy when one was terrified for one's life because one was hundreds of feet above the ground.

When finally she set him down in the massive bailey of St. Antin Abbey, he was so very thankful to have hard earth under him once more.

There was a flurry of activity as they touched down with Senia carrying Davar next to them.

It looked like the forces amassed here had fared well enough in Senia's absence. The walls still stood, though from his vantage point flying over them earlier, he'd seen the great toll those same walls had taken, pitted and damaged in many spots. The Blacklord's armies on the plains and hills to the east, a great sea of black spotted with campfires and tents, had not yet breached these defenses. It probably helped that the armies of the nations to the west had arrived.

He was taking Wyllea's word on that. Personally, he had no clue of these things and who was who, but Wyllea had pointed out the many banners amidst the sea of men camped on the hills to the west, saying they were the armies of Scandia, Nehrista, and Fjoria. These groups together did not even make a third of The Blacklord's armies, but with the stout defense of the abbey the enemy had to pass to get to them and being well fortified in the hills, Tirol guessed they could last a while.

All in all, it looked like a situation he didn't want to be in the middle of, and yet here he was. Wyllea had asked if he wished to go with her, and he'd agreed. He'd figured, correctly, that at least he'd be on the other side of the front lines—if only barely—so he could head west from here and escape this whole blasted war if he wished.

And that was the question: did he want to leave Wyllea? Did he want to be free?

Yes, he wanted to be near her... except if that meant being in the middle of a war. She had never really reciprocated his feelings. All he had to go on was that she'd said she "wouldn't leave him" after healing the wounds he'd taken from Davar. But that could mean anything. Any decent person might stick around and help a dying man. It didn't mean they loved him.

Gods, but he was confused and frustrated.

He knew he loved her, but now even that was starting to turn his emotions inside out. It was a joy to be around her, see her, talk to her, but to know that she might never see him or love him the same way burned him. He was beginning to wonder if it might not be easier to live with this unrequited love somewhere far away from her.

Even in all the time they'd had together on the way here, they hadn't talked of it. He didn't know what to say. He'd only known her for a few days! And she seemed inclined simply not to say anything. A couple of times she'd looked as if she wanted to say something, but every time it had been some mundane item or other.

He decided to do something about it now. One way or the other, no matter how she felt, she needed to know what he was feeling.

He turned to her and said, "Wyllea, I lo..." The rest of it died on his lips.

Cries of, "A scion! Another scion!" overpowered his words as a flood of people closed in around them. Suddenly, he was be pushed away from her as the horde crowded close, babbling questions all at once.

Then Wyllea was being whisked away from him. Their eyes met through the crowd for a moment, and she sent him a look of shocked confusion then a smile. She said something, her lips forming words he couldn't hear over the din of those around her. Then she was gone from view.

He sighed and shook his head. He'd missed his chance. And seeing how she was being treated now, he realized that they were just too different. She was a hero and a warrior, and he was no one. His love wasn't going to be returned. They were just not meant for one another, and he'd have to live with that.

He turned and waded through the crowd.

He stayed at St. Antin long enough for a good meal—well, three of them actually, a full day. He was still feeling a bit battered and tired from the back-to-back fights a few days ago, having come so close to death again and again. But after a full day of rest, he was feeling well enough to travel. He didn't need much. The lands west of here wouldn't be as sparse as those claimed by The Blacklord. He was a fair enough hunter and wouldn't need many provisions for the journey he planned to take. All he had to do was leave when he was ready, but still he lingered. He had hoped Wyllea would come to him, find him, but she never did.

He asked around about Wyllea. Apparently, she was meeting with the abbots and the high abbot, important people. No one seemed to know when she might be free, but in the end, it didn't matter. If she felt for him how he felt for her, she'd have found time to come to him. Frankly, he was out of energy. He didn't want to fight anymore, fight a war or fight for her. What good was it to fight for someone who'd never appreciate or reciprocate? She was lost to him, and he had to accept it.

So he found someone to show him a way out, a long tunnel deep beneath the abbey. He was told it would bring him up several hours away to the west, past even the allied armies camped above.

Yet still he waited until dusk turned to night before he left, but she didn't come for him.

So he left.

Later that night, he made a small camp in a quiet valley

between two tall rises, next to a burbling brook, with thick forest all around him. More than anything, he wanted Wyllea to be there with him, but he was joined by only stars above and a whispered breeze through the trees. He slept uneasily and moved on the next day.

CHAPTER 13

*W*yllea's life had been a whirlwind since the moment she'd landed in the bailey of St. Antin Abbey. For three days straight, she'd been meeting with monks and the high abbot. Everyone wanted her to tell the tale of her and Eaglewing. The monks were incredulous, to say the least, but they couldn't deny her scion-like abilities. Eventually, they'd relented and, in stunned awe, saw before them a future full of new Guardians. It would take generations, but they had a small hoard of the magical artifacts. If people started training with them now, then perhaps, in a hundred years or so, more Guardians might stand to defend the world against tyranny.

During this time, Wyllea had had very few, very short, moments to herself. She'd tried to find Tirol a couple of times, but the abbey was immense and she'd only managed to search a small portion of it. This search was hampered by the fact that no one she talked to seem to know who Tirol was.

Finally, after they'd dismissed her on the third day, though she'd been told to report in early the next day to begin her formal training with Eaglewing, she began a search in earnest. After an hour of futility, an idea came to her.

No one knew who Tirol was, but chances were everyone knew who and where Senia was. Indeed, the first person she asked pointed her in the right direction.

She found Senia in a small private dining chamber with a short, stern-looking, steel-haired woman and a tall young man, handsome in his way.

When Senia saw her, she said, "Wyllea, please join us."

"Actually, I was hoping you might know where Tirol has disappeared to?"

Senia's face clouded. "I don't know. I haven't seen him since the day you arrived."

"Oh." And with that, all of Wyllea's hopes fell. If Senia hadn't seen him, she had no idea who to ask to find him.

"Are you referring to the man you arrived with, the one you carried?" This from the gray-haired woman.

"Yes. Do you know where he is?"

"No," the woman said evenly, and Wyllea's hopes fell once again. "I don't know where he is now, but I know he left two days ago."

"Left?"

"Yes. I believe he was headed west."

"Oh." Wyllea closed the door to the room and simply stood in the hall for a moment. He'd left... left her.

But she had thought...

He'd been so...

Had she mistaken his affection?

No, you didn't.

Eaglewing? How do you know?

I can read minds, remember. What he felt for you was true love, my dear.

But then why would he leave?

Because love that strong, that intense, if not returned, can burn deeply.

But I... She'd meant to tell him, but she hadn't yet said anything, really. She'd always been interrupted, or too busy, or hadn't known what to say. *Oh, by all the gods, I should have found the time. I should have said something sooner. Now what will I do?*

You really need to ask?

What?

Oh, you humans and your emotions. You know what to do. You've done it before. We've been around Tirol long enough to get a sense for his unique mind. We can find him.

That's right!

She sent her senses out, flung wide to the world. She focused westward, though in truth she didn't know where he might have gone after he'd left the abbey.

Tens of thousands of minds sat on the hills to the west, but further beyond them were only a few. Dots here and there, faceless and unknown to Wyllea, except... that one.

She found him, several days to the west, sitting alone while his mind burned with desirous thoughts... of her.

Well, that definitely confirmed things.

She poked her head back into the small dining room, speaking quickly. "Tell... whoever that I might be late for my training tomorrow. I have something important to attend to."

She didn't wait for a response before running as fast as she could out of the abbey, and once free of the building, she took flight, howling through the skies of dusk.

Her desire drove her. She'd flown fast when chasing down Davar, but now she tore at the wind itself and with her powers funneled it behind her, forcing her faster and faster to the west.

What Tirol had walked in two days she spanned in an hour of swift flight.

It was full dark when she floated from the sky to land in the small clearing where he lay next to a dying fire.

He opened his eyes and slowly smiled. "This must be another dream. You're coming to me again, to be with me, to be mine. I'll take it, even if I can only ever have you in my dreams."

It was at his mention of "having her in a dream" that a thought popped into Wyllea's mind. That oh-so-real dream she'd had several days ago of being with Tirol, feeling his body, his passion for her.

I tried to tell you at the time. You were getting too close to his mind. He'd pulled you into his dream. You were there with him. It was real for you both even though it was only in his mind.

Oh... well then.

It remained only for her to tell him how she felt or perhaps, even better, show him.

"This isn't a dream, Tirol," she said as she started toward him. "I'm here. I don't know why you left, but I wanted to tell you to come back, to be with me." She held out Eaglewing and said "Guard" then released the weapon. It floated there, string pulled by some invisible hand, arrow nocked, ready to attack any unwanted intruders.

"This must be a dream," he said, rising to stand before her. "You've never been this forthcoming."

"I'm not one to express my emotions easily. That and I kept getting interrupted by people trying to kill us." She reached out, putting a hand on his cheek. With the contact, her mind linked to his, and all of his thoughts of her flashed before her. The intensity and sheer amount of his thoughts for her overwhelmed her for a moment. All of his desires, his love, his longing filled her. She drew in a shuddering breath to calm herself. "Perhaps this will show you," she said and opened her mind to his, revealing all of her thoughts of him, her own deepest secret desires.

"Oh! By all the gods!" he said, his breath clipped. "I never... oh."

His breath returned to normal, and his eyes focused on her. Then he stepped in, arms grasping her and pulling her to him. His lips found hers with a kiss so impassioned and deep it stole her breath.

She grasped him tightly, returning the kiss with all the pent-up desire she'd held within her.

He groaned, but it wasn't a pleasant sound. She released him, stepping back.

He smiled. "Blazes, but you're unnaturally strong."

"Oh, sorry. I'll try to be more gentle," she said, blushing. Gods! She never blushed.

"Don't get me wrong. I'm good with forceful, but just not quite so forceful."

She smiled. "I'll see what I can do."

They embraced again. Lips, tongues, and bodies pressing and moving together, warm in the summer's night.

The link between their minds remained, and all of their deepest secret desires were laid bare. They communicated through joined images and knew in an instant what the other longed for and needed.

She grabbed the collar of his shirt and ripped it open, tearing it fully down the front. Her hands caressed the planes of his chest, then down over the firm muscles of his torso. She slid her arms around him under the shirt, in a rough embrace. Her nails clawed at his back. His breath left him as his mind flashed images of all manner of thoughts about her... and him.

His hand pulled at her tunic, certain and unashamed. She let the shirt be removed, holding her arms above her head so he could lift it off and away.

With a grin, she tore the rest of his shirt from him as well.

"There, now we're even." She pressed against him, seeing his pleased smile at the touch of her flesh to his. "What-so-ever shall we do now?"

"No more words," he said running a hand up through her hair pushed her lips to his.

And there were no more words after that.

Well, almost no words. There were definitely some screams and yelps, some of them containing words, others just expressions of the purity of emotion between them. She was more than pleased that she was the one doing the majority of such cries. Tirol, if nothing else, was a very persistent and dedicated lover.

"Don't you want something?" she gasped, her body trembling with radiant pleasure, her breath catching and quick. Yet her mind belied her words, through their link she flashed a thousand images of her own desires.

"I'll get there in time," he teased. "Do you want me to stop what I'm doing?

"Gods no. Shut up and keep going."

He did.

There was more screaming.

Until finally he brought her to a singular moment of euphoria, tense and quivering with the intensity of her ecstasy. She'd been on top again, like that magical dream they'd shared, and after a moment she simply collapsed onto him, their lips meeting and playing at kisses as her body continued to tremble and shake with everlasting bliss.

"Gods, but you're a patient man," she breathed.

"Not anymore, I'm not." And it was his turn to be forceful.

And she'd thought she'd been screaming before... She threw her head back, moaning or screaming, too far gone into bliss to care.

And when he finally met his own rapture, they cried out together as one. Then he too collapsed into her warm embrace.

They lay there for some time as the night cooled their bodies.

Wyllea stroked some damp hair out of Tirol's face, her eyes meeting his.

"You know I love you." It wasn't a question.

He smiled. "And you know I couldn't imagine a life without you. I love you with everything I am, Wyllea."

She smiled.

He kissed her softly, sealing their union once and for all.

～

*T*irol returned to their small room in St. Antin Abbey awash in sweat. It had been weeks since they'd come back to the abbey. Wyllea trained and studied relentlessly every day, nearly all day, strengthening her Guardian abilities. So with all his free time, and having committed himself to being a part of the war against The Blacklord, he'd figured why not have some of the best warriors in the known lands teach him how to fight? It was challenging, but he was a quick study. All of his instructors had commented on his natural speed and agility, even if he did have a long way to go before he was a master of any weapon or fighting style. He enjoyed it.

His body ached, both from exertion and bruising. He was exhausted and dirty and sweaty, but even so, he smiled as he stripped off his clothes and began washing himself from the large basin in their room.

He turned as the door opened, and Wyllea stepped in.

She looked worn and tired and was only slightly less sweaty than he had been.

But when she looked up and saw him, her eyes lit and her weariness faded. She grinned broadly.

"Senia is one blazes of a sparring partner. I've never seen anyone so fast."

"You should see Master Elia or Ahrn," he replied.

"I have." She nodded. "You've got your work cut out for you." She only then seemed to notice he was undressed and let her gaze slowly take in his form.

"You're putting on muscle." A pause as her breath quickened. "Gods, but you're sexy."

With that, she released Eaglewing and came, almost literally, flying into his arms. Their lips met and he was lost in her embrace.

His heart swelled as their minds linked, their passions set ablaze.

He had found a home, a meaning, a purpose, and a love. What more could a man want?

EPILOGUE

*D*avar was alone for the first time in his life.

He'd always been separate, apart from the rest of The Blacklord's men because of his abilities and status, but he'd never been alone. He'd always had his father's presence, a voice within him, guiding and commanding him. But that was gone.

He'd studied St. Antin Abbey in preparations for the army's assault on the fortress. He knew that centuries of protection spells had been woven into these thick stone walls. And where he was now, in the deepest bowels of the fortress, those spells were the strongest.

There was no light in his cell, but he was a friend of the darkness. It was the silence, not the darkness, which terrified him most.

He knew his standing orders: capture any scion or artifact and bring it to his father; kill anyone else who got in his way. Yet that didn't help him now without Shadowfang. Oh, he was dangerous enough without his sword. His powers were still enough to take nearly anyone here, except a scion. But like most scions, Shadowfang was a part of him, and that connection was severed, at least for now, by his own magically enhanced manacles wrapped around his wrists.

They were the same ones he'd used on Senia to keep her from accessing her sword when he'd captured her, imbued with the dark magic of his father, keeping scion and artifact separated.

He didn't fear his captors. They'd try to break him, get information from him, but his will and mind were strong and he would hold. Perhaps not forever, but hopefully long enough for the armies outside to tear down these walls. Though with two scions now guarding the fortress, that outcome seemed less likely. He was also now painfully aware of the new scion's ability to tap into his mind.

He'd thought his mind impregnable. As a multitalented wizard, he could access all four of the higher domains, spirit, soul, body, and mind, and his mind talent was strongest. Yet still, a scion with mind powers would most likely be more powerful, as Wyllea had proven herself. He could hold against her for a while, but he knew now he wouldn't be able to keep her out forever. She was simply too strong.

No, his only real option was escape.

Footfalls in the hallway outside his cell and a growing light through the small grating high in his door told him someone approached.

A key slid into the lock. Perhaps his time to escape had come. Aside from the magical manacles on his hands, they had also put mundane cuffs around his ankles, chained to the wall. He had made a show of trying to break them, to settle his jailers, but he knew with his strength it wouldn't be an issue if he truly wished to snap those chains. His talent with earth magic and the ability to manipulate one's own body was nearly as strong as his mental abilities. He could surge his strength to incredible heights when he wished to.

The door opened and he stood, ready.

Then he stopped.

There in the doorway stood the most beautiful woman he'd ever seen. Pure blond hair falling in waves to just below her shoulders framed an oval face with light brown eyes that shimmered like gold in the flickering torchlight. She was tall, with a well filled out figure, not thin and willowy like Senia. No, she was shapely and curvy, full of bust and hips. She was cloaked in a long blue dress and cloak of darker blue. He'd never seen her before and had no idea why she'd be at his cell. Behind her were two burly guards.

She spoke, and her voice was a harmony of sound to his ears. "I've been asked to look in on you." There was a certain distaste in her voice. "To see if your heart is truly as black as they say."

"It is," he said with a grin.

She peered at him. It was a palpable gaze, he could feel it penetrating him, searching his soul. It wasn't an unpleasant sensation, and yet he felt somehow defenseless, violated. That wasn't right at all. If anyone was doing any violating, it should be him.

"Interesting," she said after a long moment.

"What?" What had she seen in him?

"It would seem you're not as black of soul as everyone thinks. There is good in you."

Like blazes there was!

He ripped his feet forward, tearing his chains in two quick steps. Before the guards could react, he was at the woman. She screamed as he grabbed her, turned her, one arm going around her neck. His thick bicep pushed her head back, her soft hair brushing his face. It smelled of roses.

"Either of you move, and she dies," he said, forcing his arm tighter around her neck. Her labored breathing and sounds of choking were enough to keep the two guards at bay.

"Please," she gasped, the only word she could get out. And for a moment he hesitated, his heart pricked by the plea. Never before had he had any doubt about killing an innocent if needed, but her...

He shouted at the guards. "Both of you. There is a key to these manacles. Find it or she dies!"

The guards stood there, hesitating.

"Now!" he barked, and they ran.

He waited until their footfalls and torches were distant, then released his death grip on the woman but kept his arm around her

She gasped and coughed as she regained air.

"You're coming with me, my dear." It made sense. He didn't need to kill her. A hostage might come in handy. "Try anything and you die."

It was dark in the dungeons, but that did not matter to him. He could see in darkness as in daylight, at home in shadow. Yet even without seeing her, the brush of her body so close against his sent thrills through him. He couldn't understand this. No woman had ever bewitched him like this before. He tried to block it from his mind, focus on his escape.

"Go!" he commanded.

"You aren't waiting for the key?"

"I don't need it. Besides, they'll only come back with help."

The manacles were nearly indestructible, but there was one thing that could break them, a combination of all four of the primary magical elements: earth, wind, fire, and water. True, he possessed all of these magicks, but the shackles prevented the wearer from using any magic directly on the bindings themselves. As long as he could get out of the abbey, there were wizards in the army who could help him.

Besides, he had one ability that would get him out safe. He cloaked them both in shadow, not noticeable in the darkness, but a comfort to him. As long as it was dark outside, no one would see him pass.

"I'm going to walk right out of this abbey and take you with me."

He'd been given a way out, and he would exploit it.

SCION'S SACRIFICE
The Guardians Of Light: Book 3

She'll fight for his very soul.

Davar is the son of The Blacklord, a man of pure evil. He's never questioned the wishes of his father, never even thought to go against the most powerful man in the world. He thought he was irredeemable... until he met Cass. There is something about the pure-hearted woman, and the way she sees the world and him, which

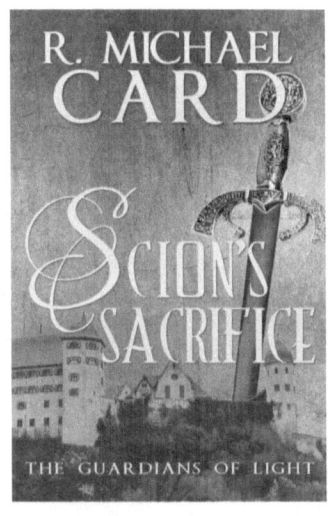

eats away at him. He doesn't want to change... or does he?

Cassine has lived a simple life, if a hidden one. She wishes only to help others, to cure the sick and wounded. As a healer for the armies that oppose The Blacklord, she's had plenty of opportunity to do so. This duty has always come first in her life and she's never had the time or desire to be with a man. But when she finds herself stranded with Davar—the enemy—she sees an opportunity to do the impossible and help him see the light within him... and to love a man who's known only hate.

*M*aster Elia rushed to the High Abbot's chambers. She wasn't pleased at having been summoned, not when she was needed out on the walls.

Outside and all around St. Antin Abbey the Blacklord's army pressed their offensive, attacking yet again, throwing ever more of their seemingly innumerable men against the fifty-foot walls and battle-ready monks of Embreth. The monks were far better trained and for every monk that fell in battle, twenty to fifty of the enemy fell. Still, Elia feared it wouldn't be enough. There were far more of the enemy than her monks.

Two factors helped to level the playing field. The first were the sisters of Ehlani, healers who could bring a monk back from the brink of death. The second and far more influential in this fight, were the two scions who battled to defend St. Antin.

Senia and Wyllea were a blessing. Two Guardians of Aehryn in an age when all were thought to be lost. Long ago The Greatest of the Gods, Aehryn of All Things, had given of herself, dying in order to bless certain people with powerful magic weapons. These special few and their descendants, or scions, became the Guardians of Aehryn. One scion was worth a hundred monks, if not more. The two women were both fierce warriors and an inspiration to her monks. She thanked Embreth for those scions every night. More recently, the armies of the west had also arrived to help. But since they were unable to fit within the confines of the abbey. They were camped in the mountains to the west. As of yet they had only sent out a few parties to skirmish with the enemy — as it was difficult to find any good battleground in the forested hills. These armies could be a great boon if they could somehow manage to coordinate their efforts.

Elia stopped before the High Abbot's door and pounded on the door.

Impatient and frustrated that she'd been taken away from helping those she'd trained and raised — her monks, her people — she tried to put on a pleasant face. She could be civil, if she wanted to be. She should be fighting, but when the High Abbot called, she obeyed. Besides, the high abbot was never disturbed or distressed, always serene. So she knew her agitation would serve her little in this meeting.

A quiet attendant ushered her into the sitting room of the High Abbot's modest suite. The room was large for private quarters, but when compared to many other rooms in the massive abbey it was still quite small. To Elia's left stood a long table with several simple wooden chairs around it. The tabletop was set with maps and papers, the defense of St. Antin. Beyond the table was a wall with a single door, which led to the sleeping chambers of the High Abbot. On the wall to her right and continuing around to the wall behind her were floor to ceiling bookshelves, filled with the High Abbot's private collection of tomes and scrolls. Before her was a large sitting area defined by a large, thick rug in front of the great hearth, which roared with a new fire. Four comfortable, well-cushioned high back chairs had been set out. Two of those chairs were occupied, one by the High Abbot herself, the other by High Sister Olinda, the ranking member of the Daughters of Ehlani in the Abbey. This made Master Elia even more curious.

She took a seat and glanced at the fourth chair, a further curiosity. Was someone else expected?

"High Abbot, if I may ask, are we waiting on another?" Elia asked, all formal courtesy despite the urgency within her to be back out on the walls in the fight.

The High Abbot of Embreth was a woman only slightly older than Elia herself, but of a much more *pleasant* look and demeanor. Where Elia knew she was short and harsh — all sharp angles and steel-gray hair with a steely attitude to match — Ullanine, the high abbot, nearly always wore a smile, which was amplified by an inner light in her sky blue eyes. She was tall and regal, and her blond hair was fading to a stark, pure, white. If Elia had cared about such things, she might have been just the tiniest bit jealous. Luckily, she didn't care. Ullanine was wise and knowledgeable and the right choice for the High Abbot.

Ullanine's smile broadened for just a moment. "Yes. I could say it's a surprise and keep you in suspense, Embreth is the keepers of secrets after all, but I won't. We await a young woman. Her name is Ragnalla of Scandia. I'm told, in their tongue, the name means 'wise counsel.' I'm hoping she will prove her name to be accurate tonight."

Elia didn't ask why three of the wisest and strongest women in their fields would need some young thing to counsel them, but she was curious. She was also curious why the scions weren't present for this meeting. The two women, even though Wyllea was still fairly new, were the center of everything done here in the Abbey.

She stayed her questions with effort, trying to remain somewhat composed. As much as she respected Ullanine's leadership, the woman's perpetual calm grated on Elia, especially now. They were at war. People were dying on the walls and still Ullanine seemed unaffected, serene. Elia was a woman formed in harsh times, in a harsh place, a woman of war and action. She'd asked the High Abbot once why she was always so peaceful and soft-spoken. Ullanine's answer had been simple: as the High Abbot, it was her job to show her faith in Embreth, to display the tranquility which comes with knowing the deeper secrets of the world, the peace of knowing all would work out, given time.

Elia wasn't so sure she believed things would work out.

So she tried to contain her aggravation and concern and relax but found it impossible. She needed to be moving, fighting, not sitting.

She glanced over at High Sister Olinda of the Sisters of Ehlani. She was younger than Elia or Ullanine, but not by much. Her hair, once soft brown waves, was now a cascade of salt and pepper framing an oval face with dark brown eyes. The woman had a sort of hawkish look with a prominent, curved nose and intense gaze. She caught Elia's look and nodded solemnly. Elia nodded back and looked away into the fire, wondering how long they would have to wait.

It wasn't long.

A knock on the door heralded the arrival of young Ragnalla, ushered in by an attendant who then promptly left, closing the door behind her.

When the young woman stepped tentatively into the light shed by the fire, Elia wondered even more at her presence. She was very young, perhaps fifteen, looking rather abashed and uncertain. She was a waif of a girl, too thin — as some girls of that age were — with long red-blond hair reaching to her thighs. The hair was pulled back from her face and braided in the Scandian style. Her face was plain, eyes brown, mouth small, nose straight. She wore a long simple dress that brushed the floor, hiding legs and feet. Not practical for fighting, but Elia suspected the girl did little of that.

She gave a fleeting smile and curtseyed. Once her hands had dropped from holding her skirt she reached for her long braid and began playing with it. It seemed a habitual action, unconscious, comforting.

"Thank you for coming, my dear," Ullanine said, her voice soft and calm. "Please have a seat." She motioned to the empty chair.

The girl sat in the chair, which seemed oversized for her. She even tucked her legs up beside her as some children did in chairs too large for them. She continued to fiddle with her braid.

Ullanine spoke, "Ragnalla has a gift. When we sought aid from the Kingdoms of the West, the Scandians were one of the first to pledge their support. When their armies marched, they brought Ragnalla with them. She does not fight, does not cook, but she has a place of honor in their ranks. She is seen as a good omen, partly because she has visions which help the army plan and prepare for the future."

Now Elia was intrigued. The True Sight was a rare and powerful gift.

Ullanine's gaze met Elia's, stern and yet hopeful. It was clear the girls gift was no trifle. "When I learned of this, I went to see the girl myself. I was skeptical of her abilities. She told me our scion would be captured. I did not think this possible given Senia's abilities and yet that came to pass. She told me we would hold within our walls at once a darkness and a great hope. I did not know what this meant, but with the arrival of Wyllea and the Blacklord's son I can see how Wyllea could be seen as a great hope for our future and the man as a great darkness. So I came to trust her abilities."

Ullanine reached across to grasp one of Ragnalla's small hands. "And now she's had another vision, but this one is different than any before. I brought her here tonight to share with you what she has seen." She turned to the girl, "Please tell us."

Ragnalla's voice was soft and hard to hear when she spoke, but with each word she gained a little confidence, enough that Elia could hear her at least. Her Scandian accent was also thick, making it harder to understand her, but Elia listened keenly so as not to miss anything. "There is a dark tide which washes against a great rock. A great light shines from the rock and will overwhelm the dark tide. Yet the ocean from which the tide came is vast and deep and at its core is a pure darkness." The girl gave an involuntary shiver before continuing. "The tide will be defeated, that is known, but after that, there are two possible futures."

Ullanine interrupted. "And that's why this vision is unlike any other. Usually, there's one clear path, but here there are two, both clear, and which will come to pass is unknown." The High Abbot's gaze was intense as it came to Elia, then passed to Olinda. Elia could sense the gravity which hung heavy over this moment. "Go on, youngling."

Ragnalla nodded. "The first of these futures is dark. The ocean is vast and deep and black and in time will swell to flood all the lands. There will be no second "dark tide," just a steady rising of water which will quench all light, covering all lands."

Well Elia certainly didn't like the sound of that. Would their fighting be for naught? Would their scions fail under the sheer power of the Blacklord? It wasn't something she wished to ponder.

"The other future is a path into the light. There are six bright fish." Ragnalla grimaced. "No, that is not right. There are five bright fish and one dark fish with only speckles of light." She stopped, shaking her head. "I am sorry, it is very hard to find the words in your language for the things I see."

"It is well, Ragnalla, we understand," Ullanine said, patting Ragnalla's hand. "Take your time."

Ragnalla nodded, taking a moment to steady herself. "There are six who must go into the heart of the ocean," she said with confidence. "Perhaps given time I can give you more details, but I know this: one who must go is of blue-fire, one is of green winds, and one is of gold and contains all the base elements. The darker one is also of all the base elements." She pressed her lips together in concentration for a moment, then shook her head. "That is all I have for now. These few and only these few must go to the depths of the black ocean, to the core. Some may not survive, but they are the only ones who have any chance to dispel the heart of the darkness. If they can do this, the dark ocean will recede from all lands and light shall prevail once more." Ragnalla's eyes gazed upon some distant sight none of the rest of them could see. Her hands had, for that brief moment, stopped playing with her braid. Then she blinked and was returned to them.

The only sound in the room was the crackle and hiss of the fire.

So there was hope. Despite the death and strife that plagued them continuously these days, perhaps there would be an end to the Blacklord within her lifetime. Elia grimaced. Did Ullanine already know such things? Was that how she managed to remain calm through it all? Yet even this sense of hope was clouded by knowing there was another equally as possible future which was far worse.

Ullanine spoke breaking the short silence. "Thank you Ragnalla, we appreciate your strength in helping us see your visions as you do. You may go now, youngling."

Ragnalla unfolded herself from the chair and with a quick bow of her head to the three older women, scurried from the room.

Elia shook her head. "Amazing." The single word seemed to hang in the air.

Ullanine looked into the fire, her hands folded in her lap, her gaze intense. "Truly," the High Abbot said, taking another long moment to ponder the flames before turning back to Elia and Olinda. "Now to our task. We must ensure that this second future comes to pass." For the first time, Elia heard an urgency in the High Abbot's voice, a break in the ever-present serenity. If she hadn't been looking for it she might not have noticed the way one hand in the High Abbott's lap grasped the other intently.

"It would seem a daunting task. How are we to know who to send?" Elia asked, starting to get curious at High Sister Olinda's silence. Unlike the other two, Elia had to move. She rose and strode toward the fire. Once there she turned to face the other two again.

Ullanine said with assurance, "I think we all know who the 'blue-fire' is."

"Senia, yes. And the 'green wind' must be Wyllea, but

who is the one of all elements. I haven't heard of such a multi-talent in generations." Elia shrugged.

"That is why I am here," Olinda said finally. The High Sister was a little too still in her chair, arms folded in her lap. It was a tranquility that came from effort, keeping oneself still.

"Oh?" Elia asked, seeing a look pass between Ullanine and Olinda. They knew something she didn't.

"One of my daughters is such a talent."

Elia knew that to be a healer of any great effect one needed the earth talent which was connected to the body. As such, most Daughters of Ehlani were earth talents to some degree. Even minor earth talents could heal most wounds. Yet someone with all elements, able to heal body, mind, soul, and spirit would be a very rare talent indeed. Elia could understand why the High Sister might want to keep this a secret.

"Her name is Cassine," Olinda said, voice measured. "And her eyes, in the right light might be said to shine like gold. The High Abbot believes Cassine is the third member of this party."

"Very well then," Elia said, "but that still leaves three members unknown, one being a 'dark one' whatever that means. How shall we know these people?" She began to pace, a short stretch back and forth in front of the fire, the heat from the hearth stimulating her into action.

Ullanine drew in a long breath. "I have been thinking about this. It is only a guess, though it feels right. But if Senia were going on any journey, who do you think would be next to her no matter what we said to him?"

Elia grimaced. "Ahrn." She nodded. Ahrn was Senia's lover and bonded mate. He was named for the Vanished God, Aehryn of All Things, who once ruled the heavens. "You're right. Most likely he will be one of those going. He would never let Senia go alone, even if it meant his death."

"Which it may," Olinda said with a sigh. "You heard what the girl said, not all of them may survive." She shook her head. "I've already brought that boy back from death's door once."

"For which he and I, and Senia are eternally grateful, High Sister," Elia said.

"Also," Ullanine went on, "if we follow that formula, then it would seem that Wyllea's man might also be another of those to go."

Elia arched a brow. "I don't see him being much help. He's only just starting his training. He has a long way to go before he'd be ready for such a quest."

"Yet from what I hear, he and Wyllea would die for each other as well and are not likely to go anywhere without the other."

Elia had to agree. "True."

"This leaves only the dark one," Olinda said.

"Yes, he or she is the mystery." Ullanine's gaze turned to the fire.

Elia had a thought. "Though if we follow the pattern, then it would be the man who loves your multi-talent," Elia said to Olinda.

"Cassine?" Olinda seemed surprised. "She has no man in her life. She is a devoted and dedicated Daughter of

Ehlani and as far as I know she's never even known the touch of a man."

Elia grimaced. That hope had died quickly.

"And so," Ullanine said, "the question remains, who is this dark one?"

Elia stopped her pacing. "Who indeed?"

CHAPTER 1

*C*assine's hope of escape vanished. She yelled for help, but her voice was drowned out amidst the din of combat and the screams of the dying all around her. The Blacklord's armies swelled around the keep in yet another night raid. She couldn't be heard and she wouldn't be seen. A magical darkness shrouded her and her captor, the Blacklord's son, as he made his way across the bailey of St. Antin Abbey toward the outer wall.

He'd captured her only moments before as she'd tended to him in the dungeons of the Abbey. He'd snapped the chains attaching him to the wall as if they'd been strings. He still wore the magical manacles that kept him from accessing his Scion-Weapon and its magic, but he was a strong multi-talent on top of his scion abilities. No one had suspected this. Only she knew. Being a multi-talent herself, she was one of the few who could see the magic within him.

He held her close in front of him. He only needed one

arm, great muscles pressing against her like a vice, wrapped around her ribcage just below her breasts. His other hand, kept close by the manacles, rested on her hip. Her feet didn't even touch the ground. Her arms were pinned, yet she could kick and thrash her head, but this seemed to affect him little.

Her heart thundered in her chest, blood boiling with an intense desire to be free of this man. But she wasn't scared, not yet. If she could find a way to escape while still within the confines of St. Antin she doubted he'd come back for her. She wasn't that important a person.

Physically she wasn't strong, but her talent with earth magic was significant and that affected the body. She stopped moving for a moment as she pumped everything she had into strengthening herself. Then she pushed away from him with all her earth-talent enhanced strength. With any normal man she would have easily pried her way out of his grip, but this was no normal man. His arm around her flexed as she tried to escape and she succeeded only in freeing one arm before he yanked her back, tight to him. His earth talent was amazing! A moment later he'd caught her free arm and was pinning it to her side once again.

"You are a feisty one aren't you?" A deep baritone rumbled from within him.

Her stomach clenched in panic, blood pounding in her ears. She was losing time, but she had so much more at her disposal than just her earth-talent.

Unable to see through the darkness around her, Cassine sent out her life-sense. There were many others around, dashing through the bailey or lying too still as their life-essence faded. Yet she found it hard to sense those nearby as her life-sense was half-blinded by her captor's brilliant bloom of life energy. No wonder he'd been able to overpower her earth-talent enhanced strength. He was a potent individual, powerful in many respects, physically for sure, but the pure power of spirit within him was like a beacon in the night. This shook her to her core and nearly overwhelmed her. She doubted any of her magic would affect him. He was simply far too powerful.

Her strongest talent was with water and soul magic, but there was little that could do to him, except dishearten him perhaps. She tried to push at his soul, making him doubt himself, uncertain. Yet she found his soul to be an inky, oily place which disgusted her.

He hesitated for just a moment, her effects on him clear, but his determination to escape was too strong and he was moving again a moment later.

Her thoughts danced, frantic. Her heart raced, trapped in her chest like she was trapped in this man's arms. His pure life energy would give him away in an instant to any who were looking for it, but no one else here, even either of the scions, could see life as she could. Cassine's life-sense was an ability of water and soul. It was enhanced by her link to fire and spirit as well as to earth and the physical body, but she doubted anyone else could see things the same way. If Senia was nearby she might become aware of this man's spirit, which was incredibly strong, but Senia was likely out beyond the walls fighting, and it might be too late by the time she caught up with them.

Cassine's terror bloomed into a black cloud of doubt and fear. She now felt what she'd been trying to make him feel. How could she ever hope to escape this man?

"Please," she tried one last time. "Don't do this. I know there's good in you." She had seen it. His soul might have been a twisted, dark thing, but mixed into the warped wounds was more than one strand of empathy, of kindness. They might not be large, nor many, but they were there.

"There is no good in me," he growled, his voice a low, deep and husky.

"Perhaps you can't see it, but I can."

He tightened his grip on her, his free hand moving up to grasp her throat, choking her. "Speak of this again and you'll know how evil I am."

Despite his words, he released her neck. He could have killed her, yet he hadn't.

He crouched and leapt. They were close to the walls. The life-essences of those in the bailey stopped abruptly. She felt the rush of warm wind on her face, tousling her long hair.

His leap took them well above the fifty-foot walls, the life essences of those on the wall sinking farther and farther below them.

She'd hoped he wouldn't take her this far, that he'd discard her before this, but he hadn't. She had to do something quickly or she'd be neck deep in the Blacklord's armies. He alone was bad enough, but there were other mages serving the Blacklord as well and she'd have little hope once she was in amidst all of that magic. She trembled, yet still some core of strength within her sought for a way out, something to save her.

She couldn't affect him, so she needed to do something else, but what?

There was one thing.

She'd only ever done it once before and that had been by accident nearly twenty years ago as a child.

Yet she knew it was possible and she remembered how it had felt, the memory ingrained into her being. It took all elements and a great deal of power. She had no idea if it would work, but it was her only hope, the only magic she could think of to free herself. Desperation pushed her. She had to try, even if she had no clue what would happen. She knew only if she stayed with this man she couldn't imagine a worse fate.

She tried to calm herself as he began his descent, gathering her energies. First, she drew upon water, her most significant talent. She felt her own blood, the liquid life within her as well as the aura that was her soul. These were like her hands or face, so well known to her as to be taken for granted. Then she gathered her strength in earth, her second strongest talent, the ability to heal, which had gotten her into the Daughters of Ehlani. She used the knowledge of the body to strengthen her muscles and harden herself for what was to come. Next was fire and spirit, closer to soul than mind, but still not a strong element for her. She reached out with her spirit to a distant place, sensing the world around her, knowing the feel of all things, as spirit was the element that created and connected all things. Finally air, her weakest element and connected to the mind. She calmed her thoughts, ready now for the extreme effort she needed to push herself out of her own being, taking mind, body, soul and spirit with her to another place in an instant.

The only problem was, she couldn't control where she went.

She felt the tearing of the fabric of reality as she pushed herself to some other, distant place. Her body would have been torn apart if not for the earth magic she'd pushed into it. There was disorientation and pain. It was incredibly intense, but only for an instant. There was a cry, from whom, she didn't know, she was a being of magic at the moment and the needs and sensations of her body were distant. She floated free, detached, in all places at once and none. The sensation lasted a mere heartbeat and yet stretched for an eternity, one breath drawn out for what seemed like hours.

She landed, feeling solid earth under her feet. She'd done it. Her soul elated, celebrated. She was free!

Snapping out of the trance she'd needed to teleport herself, she came to her senses despite her entire being: body, soul, mind, and spirit, feeling drained and weak.

Instantly she realized something had gone wrong.

When she'd done this as a child, she'd been alone. This time, she hadn't been, and somehow she'd taken her captor with her.

By all the Gods, no!

Yet even as her heart sank, his grip loosened and

released. He fell to the ground behind her with a heavy thud. She wanted to run away, to cry out with joy, but with her own weakness she couldn't do anything but collapse to her knees. She sat there for a moment, still trying desperately to get up, away from this place and that man.

There was no strength in her however. She doubled over onto her hands.

Perhaps she could crawl.

Instead, she found herself taking several long, deep breaths to keep from blacking out. It wasn't enough. She sank to the ground as everything slowly went dark.

For a moment, her mind still functioned before unconsciousness took her. One thought circled in her mind: she lay in some unknown place with her captor still close by. The Gods must hate her.

TALES OF THE SEVEN KINGDOMS

The Goblin King

The Swordmaster's Apprentice

GUARDIANS OF LIGHT

Book 1: The Last Scion

Book 2: Scion Rising

Book 3: Scion's Sacrifice

ABOUT R. MICHAEL CARD

R. Michael Card has loved fantasy since he read his first Dragon Lance book so many years ago. He has been writing for twenty years, but has only recently decided to start sharing his work with the world. He has always enjoyed the lighter side of epic fantasy, the grand adventure, and has infused that love into his works.

He lives near Toronto Ontario with his beloved wife and their cat. He has had a plethora of careers, working in software, insurance, trades, and education, with jobs ranging from washing cars to career counseling.